Special Th
Allison St
Holli Carlo
Kerry Ste
Reinhard E
Jack & Gale Wallace, Mitch Ballou, Julie Racowski,
Barbara and Larry Stewart, Ethiopian Consulate,
Saudi Arabian Air Force, Central Intelligence
Agency, Mike Harris, Rev. Michael Meyers, Spanky.

Library Of Congress
Catalogue p113097
Copyright 1998, Reignbow Marketing Inc.
The Voice, Brian Stewart

Author's note:
The author in no way wishes to offend anyone of
any religious persuasion whether it be Jew,
Christian, Coptic, Muslim, Catholic or otherwise.
Acts by individuals characters should not reflect
upon the general good caused by faithful adherants
to above mentioned religions. God is first and
foremost love and anyone who acts in love acts
according to God's precepts just as anyone who acts
out of any other motive acts contrary to God's will.
The use of the name "Allah" is referenced to one of
the original statues found in the pagan shrine Kaaba
and not the modern day reference to Allah as
believed to be by most Moslems the name of the
Most High God.

The Voice

There's a Voice that you've heard all your life.
Telling you what was wrong or right.
But you lie to yourself and it goes away.
And you wish it would have stayed..

You're sad because your life's gone amiss.
You know that the Voice is what you miss
You still long for the love and you long for the sound
But the Voice you can't find because it's not around.

So you take up a cause or swallow a pill
But the void that's within can never be filled.
And you wonder where you careened off the road.
Cause the Voice that said "Stop." You just ignored.

In the pages you read that lie just ahead.
Is the story of the Voice you thought was still dead
Step away from the madness the broad road to doom.
Listen for the Voice that will speak the truth.

THE VOICE

by

Brian Stewart

CHAPTER ONE
The Rocks Cry Out

Detroit resembled Berlin after being leveled by the Allies near the conclusion of World War II. All the city blocks that had been destroyed in the riots of the 60's, still lay desolate in the noonday sun. Only the rats scurried to and fro undisturbed except by the ever increasing population of alley cats, cats every bit as cunning as the most feared man-eating tigers that still ravaged the small villages of India. Automobiles, stripped bare of chrome, windows, doors, seats, radios, stood up on concrete blocks looking like Death Valley skeletons eaten clean as the carrion of the decaying post-industrial infrastructure. America's thriving automobile industry had built the city and the desertion of the industry to greener pastures had left it's former hub in the gutter along with many of the children of the first autoworkers. Those who could had moved out, others strapped without transportation, education or direction had stayed. Most lived in hopelessness.

There in the midst of the rubble and inner city turmoil, stood the one bright light - WOC - World Outreach Center. It stretched out nearly a city block beaming it's bright light, one beacon of hope for a neighborhood that had long ago sunk into utter hopelessness. The entire city block had been donated by a local bank that had been holding the deed so long they had jumped at the opportunity to just get rid of it. Matching Federal funds had helped pay for the school and studio which trained inner-city youth in the fine art of broadcasting. Jack Wallace the thirty-something minister had run a construction company in Vail, Colorado until, in the middle of the night he had seen a strange light in the corner of his hilltop chalet. He rubbed the sleep out of his eyes and fell to his knees. It was the very presence of the Mighty One. The message he received was one word - Detroit.

It had been several busy years since he had answered the call and had gotten off the plane and driven his rented car through the city, only to be stabbed fourteen times. He realized then that Detroit was more dangerous than any place in the world. With each thrust of the knife from the gang members intent on stealing his wallet full of credit cards and less than forty dollars cash, came the impetus to follow the call. He liquidated his construction company, houses, jeeps, emptied his pension plan, stock market accounts and showed up in Detroit with a dream and enough seed money to get it off the ground.

The church was in the heart of the ghetto, near the spot where he had been mugged. He managed to get it built and full in only fourteen months, using used television broadcasting equipment and working on the construction himself, breaking his back nearly sixteen hours a day only stopping when his Irish wife Gale showed up with homemade bread and soup for the crew. Because of the area, the city waived building inspection permits and he was pretty much permitted to build as he pleased. Consequently, the building ceiling was nearly sixty five feet high and featured a heliport on top. The plans were given to him bit by bit in dreams and visions. Drew Tonney, his best friend from Kansas State and former business partner, did the architectural renderings and designed the landscaping. It was truly an oasis.

The local television stations covered the progress as well, and the newspapers did several features on the story drawing curiosity seekers who began filing by. People called from all over wondering if they could help. As he had promised, the Mighty One had sent His people to help unfold the vision. Paul Kimble, a retired television executive, signed on to start the school and within sixty days had recruited enough students to make the broadcast college a reality. Even though the equipment was not state-of-the-art, it was adequate enough to provide as full a range of training as any of the kids could have achieved at even the prestigious USC. They also built enough adjoining space for a local philanthropist who had won a Nobel prize for scientific research to establish a full state of the art research center.

Daily chapel was mandatory and the permeation of the pure

word of God breathed through Jumpin' Jack Flash's sermons quickly won over all the kids. They lobbied for more Bible studies and most of the students began attending the Sunday morning services and inviting others as well. The church auditorium was able to hold several thousand with the services taped and put on the free access channels all over the United States. Several of the kids bugged Paul until he allowed them to translate the shows into Polish, Lithuanian, Amaharic and French. Broadcast tapes were sent all over the world. Jumpin' Jack Wallace was not one to be taken lightly. Not only was his voice thunderous but he was a former triathelon champion. If it hadn't been for an injury sustained in college football, many believe he would have been a gold medalist, for he could run, jump and throw with the best. To illustrate a point oftentimes he would run across stage and jump over the row of chairs on the platform barely nicking the tops of them and telling the congregation that those of them who were backslidden and living in sin had a slimmer chance of going to Heaven. It was Fire and Brimstone delivered theatrically and the people drove from all over the Midwest to meet, shake hands and have their babies prayed for by Jumpin' Jack who would stand outside every morning after service. The more the visitors came the larger the offerings grew until the World Outreach Center coffers were full and all the debts were paid off. The Broadcast School purchased their own full power VHF station and satellite uplink that reached across into Canada and allowed their broadcast to be picked up globally. The film school had a full animation department that was producing Christian children's videos, but it still wasn't enough. Jumpin Jack wasn't going to stop until he had helped carry out the great commission - Preach the gospel to every living soul and to that cause he gave his every breath.

Gale Wallace was far from idle. Not only was she a good wife, she was as enthusiastic in her ministry as Jack was in his. She believed God had called her and raised her up to reach young single women by getting them dependant solely on God for their emotional needs, weaning them away from relying on any man. She taught them how to pray, lead their family members to Christ and advised caution against yielding to the lusts of the flesh. She advised the girls not to date, but to depend on God through prayer to bring them their husbands. She told them there was nothing wrong with kissing, but it just led to other things including immorality which was displeasing to a Holy Pure God. Her fellowship group, the Holy Women of God, was a thousand strong with women praying for women sometimes until the wee hours of the morning. Each week more and more women were drifting in to pray for their lost sons, spouses and found the fellowship so rich that the services usually were the highlights of their week.

Julie Reinhold, a single woman, was one of the most faithful members of Gale's group. She had experienced the pain of rejection directly relating to her sin of fornication while she had been engaged to Tim McDonald a promising young Ford Motor Executive. He had talked her into consummating their relationship four months prior to their set marriage date. She had felt guilty after giving in to him the one time and repented before God, and steadfastly refused his other advances. The spirit of lust controlled his heart and had him baying like a dog desirous of any female companionship. She caught him in bed with a fellow worker one afternoon and left his condominium in tears. Betrayed and humiliated, she had joined Holy Women of God at her mom's insistence and found herself truly enjoying the fellowship. Her degree in Communication and Applied Science and Engineering made her a perfect candidate to run the Communication and Computer Division of World Outreach University. Two years had passed and she had forgotten about Tim and began to think of herself as married to God. She knew God had someone for her and she was quite content to wait until he came along.

Julie joined Gale for lunch at their favorite coffee shop, The Black Bean, and was in a heavy discussion when her mobile phone rang.

"I can't get you right now." She said into the phone. "Yea. I'll meet you there about five o'clock."

She hung up the phone and put it back into her purse and turned and smiled at Gale

"It's my brother. He's brought home a friend of his from Israel and he wants me to meet him."

"What's the guy's name?" Gale asked.

"Ben Gibron." Julie answered reflecting on his picture, a true Maccabbean hero. "He' s knockout. He has piercing blue eyes and stands six foot three. With soldiers like that it's no wonder six millions Jews can't be defeated by two hundred million Arabs."

"One plus God is a majority." Gale smiled.

"I know." Julie answered. "Look I don't know if I'm really ready to meet anybody at all. I feel like there's a battle inside of me. I totally hate Tim for what he did. I can't even stand looking at a picture of him. When I think about him it's mostly weird thoughts like watching him being tortured. I truly hate him for what he did."

"You've got to let go of your hatred and let God help you forget, you could be blocking a blessing God wants to bring in your life. Marriage is a blessing for me and could be for you as well, but for a woman who gets married with any hate at all in her heart, Solomon says she's dangerous." Gale prayed silently for the right words to tell her best friend. "God is going to use the situation with Tim to show you His forgiveness. Forgive us our trespasses as we forgive those... Look behind you. Isn't that Tim pulling up in the Continental?"

Julie looked over. Her heart sank. With him was Vicki Petrollio, the girl he had cheated with. There was no escape, he was coming in their favorite spot with his new girl. The world was too small for both of them. Tim walked right up to her.

"Hi Jules." He smiled sensing the pain and trying to be casual about it. "You've met Vicki haven't you?"

Julie looked at him. "How could I forget her." She broke out laughing and went into hysterics. Gale sat stunned and Julie couldn't keep a grip on her emotions.

"Look," Julie tried to regain her composure. "I'm not laughing at you. I'm just laughing at the irony. You cheated with my fiance and now he's bringing you to our old hangout. Tim, I would have thought an Advertising Executive for Ford Motor company would at least have had a more creative idea than that."

Julie reached inside for strength from the Mighty One. "Tim, I've really hated you for what you did. You ruined my life, took my virginity and then cheated on me just a short time before my wedding date, but I forgive you. I'm not going to hate you anymore because I know if I do it's just going to eat away at me bit by bit until there's nothing left of me. So good luck to both of you."

Vicki and Tim walked away in shock. Julie sank her face into her hands and looked up at Gale.

"I don't know what came over me." Julie said. "It was like a spirit of joy, of relief that God had showed me what kind of man he really was before I married him."

"I'm proud of you." Gale said, "and as far as him taking away your virginity, I really believe the Mighty One has restored it within you. Remember the old things have passed away and all things have become new. Surely that applies to sex as well..."

"You're right!" Julie said, finishing her coffee and marvelling at how relieved and at peace she felt within.

Her brother Doug still held on strongly to his Catholic beliefs. He went to church confession regularly. Rather than enter into the priesthood as everyone thought he would after his years at Holy Cross College in Worcester, Massachusetts, he had opted for a Master's in Archaeology and was busy digging up artifacts from the Biblical time periods. He had met Ben while in Ethiopia looking for the Ark of the Covenant that Menilek, King Solomon's son by Sheba had brought back with him after learning the Jewish religion in Jerusalem. It was rumored to be located in St. Catherine's in Asmar the Northernmost part of the country but many scholars believed the copy they had on display and brought out for their yearly processionals for the Coptic religion was not the real thing. Ben, on grant from the Jerusalem Art Museum, was looking for the same thing and they had decided to team up. Ben was interested in bringing it back to Jerusalem to use in the temple which he believed was going to be rebuilt. Doug's interest was purely scholarly and funded by a large Catholic run insurance trust that assembled religious articles to display around the world. Doug was on grant from one of their oldest benefactors, a wealthy African-American who wanted to restore pride to the African race by showing them their cultural heritage. They were both glad for a break away from the poverty of Ethiopia and were exhausted by their search. They knew it would be a miracle to make a discovery so monumental, but each of them believed it was possible.

Julie pulled into her parent's driveway anxious to meet Ben. Doug hadn't been away long enough for her to miss him really badly. She stopped and looked in the rear view mirror wondering if at twenty-nine she was growing into an old maid. Wondering if she'd ever find anyone to marry, or for that matter someone who could just be depended on to tell her the truth. Before she got out of the car Red and Tallow, her family's golden retrievers, jumped on her nearly knocking her over and getting their muddy paws all over her white silk dress from Jessica McClintock. Her father hobbled over leaning heavily on his cane.

"Julie." Her father greeted, his skin as pallid as a freshly dug up corpse denied the life giving atmosphere of our planet. " Come here give your old man a hug."

Julie looked over at him surprised at how fast his once robust health had degraded. She had heard that heart attacks were hard on people but it was the first time she had ever seen the before and after in such a first hand way.

"Red. Tallow. " Julie commanded firmly. " Go sit." They obeyed." Hi dad." She greeted him with a soft kiss on his cheek. "How are you feeling?"

"It takes a licking and keeps on ticking." John Reinhold

grinned and tapped his chest. "Look I know You've been delaying your fellowship in Jerusalem because of my health. I criticized you pretty heavily about your assignment but I want you to feel free to go. I've lived my life I don't want you waiting around Detroit for me to die. I know I haven't followed the Good Lord much but maybe He'll give me a few more years. We're on the list for a new heart and when I get it if it goes all right...It's pretty gruesome Isn't it? Someone has to die so I can live."

"Dad, that's how it's always been. Jesus died so you can live eternally." Julie looked at him with compassion.

"Now Julie. I know how you feel about your religion but I've already lived my life and really I'm not into that Jesus thing. Your mom and I have always gone to church and I've been a good person. If that doesn't count for something then I guess I'll just have to take my chances."

"Dad." Julie started to get exasperated. "It counts for something but you've still got your pet sins. God can't allow you in Heaven with any sins. The Bible says. "If we confess our sins He will forgive us." Jesus stands at the door of your heart and knocks. He doesn't want you just going to church, He wants to have a relationship with you everyday. Jesus is not just my God, Dad. He is my husband. When I travel He keeps me company. When I'm lonely I can pray and He's right there with me. It's awesome, Dad. I wish you could feel how I feel inside."

A glow had enveloped Julie and her father looked at her wondering why his daughter seemed as a light in the fog just beaming with energy. He felt its warmth and was drawn to the love inside her. His heart, hardened from years of doing things his own way, began to crack a little bit as the light of the truths she spoke seeped into him.

Just as he was about to respond his wife called out.

"John. You and Julie come in. Ben's here."

"We'd better go in." Her dad said. "We can talk more about this later."

The Voice

"Dad it's best to make your peace with God while the spirit of God is still calling you."

Julie always felt comfortable in her parents house full of antiques. The grandfather clock her great grandfather had brought over from Germany was the focal point of their well decorated living room full of priceless furniture. The couches and chairs her mom had custom upholstered and their vintage Mason & Hamlin grand piano, at which she had studied so long when she was young thinking she'd be a concert pianist, filled a nice spot in the front window showing both signs of wear and care. She stopped for a minute and played an especially difficult section of Rachmaninoff C-sharp piano concerto. Ben walked in, sat next to her and helped her finish the piece. By the time they had reached the ending the whole family had gathered around with her brother clapping boisterously and yelling. "Encore."

"You play well." She said, giving Ben a warm embrace. "I didn't know Rachmaninoff had ever written for four hands."

"I don't suppose he ever did." Ben replied returning the smile. "I don't suppose that he ever wrote for hands as rusty as mine either. My travels don't permit me to play on a regular basis."

"Jules." Doug interjected taking advantage of the momentary lull between them. "What's this I hear about your fellowship going through? You're going to Jerusalem to find the Voice of God?"

Everyone looked at her with strange expressions.

"It was supposed to be a surprise Doug. How'd you hear?" Julie was mad that her big announcement had been treated so irreverently.

"Julie, You're leaving now?" Her mom looked hurt.

"I haven't fully decided, Mom. A grant that I applied for to do some applied physics in the Holy Land came through. Three hundred thousand in funding. It's from the Guggenheim Foundation for the advancement of Religious studies."

"What is it you hope to find." Ben asked. "The Voice of God?"

"Yes. My thesis was written on Drift Reduction Multiple Time

Sampling. Instead of Carbon dating rocks for age, we will be running rock samples through complex computerized photo detectors and looking for frequencies not common to this planet."

"Where do you plan on getting your rocks?" Doug questioned.

"We already collected some from Mt. Sinai. The Bible says that God spoke to Moses there. Just think, if science can provide irrefutable evidence like the finding of Noah's Ark or the lost cities of Ninevah and Babylon or the Voice of God more people will believe."

" I don't think you're going to be able to separate God's voice from the other sounds held in the rocks from Mt. Sinai. There is just bound to be too much stored in them to be able to pull them out; thunderstorms, lightning strikes; but if you could find an artifact like the original tablets of Law, say, inside the Ark of the Covenant, not only would they possibly contain the Voice of God but the book of Exodus says they were written by the very hand of God. If somehow you could use your same equipment to show that the very words on the slabs of stone were somehow engraved in by an instrument that didn't even exist in those times. You could prove to the world that God Almighty Jehovah really did give us the Ten Commandments and truly exists."

"That sounds really plausible." Julie said reflectively."It sounds well within the grant I have applied for too, but what are the odds of me ever getting hold of the original Ten Commandments?"

"Pretty good." Doug smiled. "We've been on the track of them for some time and have got them narrowed down to a small area in Ethiopia. Why don't you come with us. It's not that far from Jerusalem."

"Julie. Don't stay behind to care for me. Go." Her father added. "You've got your own life to lead, I've got your mom to look after me and she's been doing a really good job for the last twenty-eight years. Speaking about doing a good job, I can smell the food now. We'd better take our seats before everything gets cold."

The woods behind their house was full of moss covered rocks, and tall majestic oak trees covered with vines and more wildlife than the rain forest jungles. It was a place that Julie had always called her magical forest. She had played her entire life in the forest and was anxious to show it to Ben.

"Doug." Julie yelled from the kitchen, helping her mom clean the supper dishes. "I'm going to show Ben the forest. We'll be back in about an hour."

Ben marveled at how thick the woods grew just in the Reinhold's backyard. It was another world to him. There was a fallen oak tree in a clearing with a stream of light coming down as if it were a spotlight aimed by the Creator. Julie held her hand up to direct Ben's attention to the young fawn looking warily about, eating the long grass that grew beneath the stump of the tree. A squirrel clambered down the tree trunk, picking up the acorns and stuffing them in his cheeks, instinctively preparing for the long winter still months and months away. Ben moved and the deer looked over. They locked eyes and Ben approached it stealthily. Before he got within twenty feet the deer bounded away and the squirrel bolted.

"God must have given them the common sense to be wary of men. If the wind had been blowing behind us we would have never gotten that close. They can smell predators miles away." Julie said.

"That's what you think of mankind, a race of predators? The rich devour the poor, the strong rule over the weak?" Ben questioned.

"Look at your own country."Julie pointed out. "You are a Jew living with about six million other Jews surrounded by two hundred million Arabs who would love to blow you and all your countrymen to shreds. Over what? a piece of land that was a wasteland inhabited by a few shepherds for almost two thousand years? I'd say that was pretty predatory."

"I'd probably agree with you." Ben responded. "I still don't like to think of myself as a predator. Even when I did my time with the Israeli Air Force. When I shot down the Russian built MIGS, I

The Voice

wasn't thinking of the strong versus the weak. I was just protecting my homeland."

"Your territory." Julie added.

"Right! My territory, and also the defenseless women and children that lived in our Kibbutz. I was their protector." Ben's mind drifted back to the missiles he had to fire on the fighter jet and the thrill he felt when he watched the missile lock on and destroy the invading aircraft.

"Did you enjoy it?" Julie looked at him giving him no chance to do anything but tell the truth.

"Yeah." Ben spoke. "I was a better pilot and our jets and missile tracking devices were better. I was proud that I had defended my country."

"You never thought about the man that you sent plunging into eternity?"

"No." Ben said. "He made his choice when he chose to get in the plane and attack us. He knew the odds and they beat him. What are you getting at?"

"Nothing." Julie laughed. " All you Israeli's think it's your weapons, your planes, your training, your technology but none of you see what it really is. It's your God who has chosen to fight for you and defeat your enemies. Aren't you familiar with any of the prophets? They wrote that God was going to scatter His people and bring them back out of the very graves. Think about the first inhabitants of your country, concentration camp survivors, prisoners from the gulags of Siberia and the north. I'm not saying your people are not brave and intelligent, but it is obvious to anyone who reads the Bible that there is a God working on your behalf, a savior that the leaders of your people abandoned when they thought the Messiah should have come with a show of force to run out the Romans instead of as Isaiah prophecies as a suffering servant to be the Lamb of God and die for the sins of the world just as the passover lamb was slain to protect the first born in Egypt right before the first great Exodus."

13

"So you believe my people rejected the true Messiah and consequently God rejected them?"

"Yes." Julie stated." Look at what happened less than one generation after they rejected the first followers of Jesus. The Romans came and scattered the people and destroyed the temple of Solomon, literally pulled it apart brick by brick as the gold ran between it's cracks. For nineteen hundred years they were a nation of wanderers driven from one country to another until 1948 when Palestine became Israel."

"You really do believe in Jesus don't you? You believe He was the Messiah?"

"He was." Julie added. "Sometime, I'll go through all the prophecies that were foretold about Him and He fulfilled."

"Okay." Ben said looking at her. "I'll be open minded. Now show me more of your woods before it gets dark and they've got to send a rescue party out for us. On second thought I don't think it would be too bad, being trapped out here with you anyway."

"It's not going to happen." Julie answered. "This way, there's a small hill where you can look over everything."

CHAPTER TWO
Money To Burn

Prince Farshad was eight times removed from the royal throne of Saudi Arabia. So it was a sure bet that he would never rule over the vast desert kingdom mostly inhabited by foreigners brought in to build the superstructures financed by the huge oil reserves. Although educated at Harvard and afterwards Edwards Air Force Base, he had never developed a tolerance for the Jewish race or westerners in general. He admired their women as beautiful, strong and independent, but he hoped for their annihilation. He was willing to give his life to an all out Jihad or Holy War and viewed his cousin who ruled the throne as weak and vacillating, far more concerned about economics than Muslim politics. Farshad was the only member of the royal family that kept close ties with Iran's ruling elite. He used his vast wealth to finance many splinter terrorist groups and to monitor events in the Holy City of Jerusalem lest it be totally wrested away from the followers of Mohammed.

He watched with alarm the Jews' plans to rebuild the Temple of Solomon and knew if they ever succeeded, the Muslim mosque Dome of the Rock, which had stood on the former Jewish Temple site for centuries, would be destroyed.

He looked over the vast desert kingdom as his pilots flew him in his converted 727 to Addis Ababa where he was checking on his vast holdings of hotels, factories and farms. In the cockpit, the pilot Steven Dragoon radioed his approximate arrival time hoping that the air controllers at the small international airport had a landing slot scheduled. He had at first detested the African way of bribes, kick backs, long waits, but after he had learned the system and how to get what he needed for the plane and crew, he had become quite adept at playing it. He looked over at the co-pilot and navigator for whom he had nothing but disdain.

Quentin Girard, the co-pilot, was thirty-five and also an arrogant Frenchman who fit the prototype exactly. Loud and unfriendly, he carried himself with an aura of vast superiority bolstered by the fact that he was chief pilot for one of the wealthiest men in the world. He was a womanizer, a drunk and could barely keep one paycheck ahead of his bills, blowing his huge salaries pretending he was a high roller like the Prince. Steven wondered how long it would be before he lost his head or became an incident.

Jack Owens, also a qualified pilot and another crew member, was another story. He was a solid dependable graduate of the Air Force Academy dismissed when he could no longer pass the rigorous physical. He had been a godsend, someone Steven could truly call his friend. He viewed his job with pride and went about it in the most professional way. He had a young wife and four children manning the homestead in Melbourne, Florida just downwind from Cape Kennedy. At first it was hard on him, month on month off, but he had adapted well to the requirements of his professional life and after serving together on the crew for three years, they had become fast friends.

"Jack." Stephen questioned."We've got a strong tail wind. Can you calculate a new arrival time?"

"No problem." Jack answered on his headset microphone, checking the various controls and charts. "What do you suppose they'll charge us to land this time? They're getting more and more desperate for foreign currency."

"Their money's not worth squat." Quentin interjected. "C'est mere."

"Don't give us any of your fancy French expressions, besides Quentin, you haven't saved a hundred francs in these last three years. If you didn't have a paycheck coming in every week you'd be in just as bad a shape as the lot of them"

"Maybe so," Quentin smiled. "But I make up for it by drinking plenty of champagne so I don't remember what I spend."

"Well someday", Jack added, "you're going to be old and then you're going to wish you had saved for that rainy day. Don't come crying to me for a handout or show up at my door."

"In Florida," Quentin was delusional, "I'll win big and retire in Monaco, maybe buy a place next to Prince Albert. Don't worry your head about me. I'll be fine."

The airport was crowded with people carrying packages and large oversize bags from Europe, United States. Almost nothing was made in Ethiopia and nearly everything except coffee and other food items was imported. A limo was waiting to take the prince to his mountaintop estate and a van to take the crew to the Hilton. As they walked out to the van, Jack looked around and thanked God that his family didn't live on the edge of poverty and starvation like so many in Ethiopia.

None of them even noticed the Lufthansa Airliner that landed moments later carrying Ben, Julie and Doug. She had agreed to come with them prior to her trip to Jerusalem. She'd already begun to fall in love with Ben, so not too much talking was necessary. Ben looked over her lap as they were landing.

"You won't be able to escape your feelings of helplessness." Ben stated. "When you see all these kids on the streets begging, it'll make you pretty ill."

"Why can't we just buy them all something to eat?" Julie said naively.

"You'd need a transport full." Doug interjected. "They're everywhere, eyes bugging out and hands motioning for you to feed them. Tattered clothes, no shoes; the worst are the two and three year olds. Most of the people here just walk by them. They become invisible. You'll start feeling guilty for being so rich."

"I'm not rich." Julie defended herself.

Ben held her wrist. "Your watch costs more then they make in their lifetime. You're rich, We're all rich compared to them."

The plane bounced down and taxied in. A feeling of dread came over Julie and she didn't know why. It was a mixture of excitement and fear of the unknown. She realized she had stepped into the jaw of death to pursue her dream and she wondered if it was worth it or if it would have been better just staying home.

Moussaud Hadidsian's eyes darted back and forth scanning the passengers that had departed from the Detroit/Hamburg flight. He was paid to let nothing slip by. He was dressed in a simple turban and flowing gown and smoked a hand-rolled cigarette. He was nervously blowing out smoke, ring after ring. It was a skill he had learned in a Parisian prison before he had been traded back to Iran for some important French Secret Agents. He didn't have the faintest idea where the funding came for him to continue his surveillance but he knew that the Israeli and his American friend were up to no good and that the ancient temple artifact they were so obviously looking for in Ethiopia would be better left unfound. Either way whether they found it or not he had decided not to let them live. He laughed at how inadequate the x-ray technology used at the airport was at detecting the new Teflon bullets and plastic gun hidden under his robe.

He despised his director's order to let them live until they found the artifact and looked at his watch wishing he was in the mosque and could pay his homage to Allah as was his custom five times a day. If he could have, he would have stayed in Mecca, but he knew true devotion was the destruction of the infidels and their decadent way of life and to that end he was truly devoted. Car bombs, terrorist attacks on bus stations, hospitals, he had done them all. The only good infidel was a dead infidel. He looked forward to the day when the followers of Allah ruled the earth and all the rest of mankind was either dead or subjugated as slaves. He had no use for the ways of the west or the east and despised wholly the African way of bribery and inefficiency. He had no idea where the hate and intolerance that ruled his spirit had originated from. When he was younger he had learned that Allah desired his worship and that there was no better way to worship than offering to him blood sacrifices. While in military training school he had been invited to enter a select group of promising young people from influential families. Since his father was a ranking member of the Shamshir Siah, it was only natural that he would follow in his footsteps. He learned that mercy and love were for the weak and that the strongest survived at the expense of the weakest. The group leader Alloh Khachatorian was close to seventy years old and had learned the black Arts while on travels to Tibet. He felt the power he had amassed only made his devotion to Mohammed and the Koran stronger and assured him a place in the Paradise his religion taught him waited for all the faithful followers of Islam. He couldn't have been more wrong.

Moussaud's stomach had turned the first time he watched a live human sacrifice. It was a young girl from a neighboring town. Her parents were poor herdsmen and had bargained her away as a domestic worker for the school. Twelve of the young novitiates to the Black Guard gathered around as Alloh prepared her for the sacrifice. They had a large stone altar with chains at the top and bottom where they secured the young girl who, being drugged by her coffee, had no idea of the ritual they would be putting her through. The leader defiled her for a moment and encouraged each of the boys barely sixteen to do so as well. Moussaud still had a hard time erasing the glazed look in her eyes. Her wrists were slit and she was slowly bled into different jeweled chalices. Alloh gave them each small scimitars with handles encrusted in rubies, each ornately carved and smithed out of the finest gold and steel. One by one they approached the body and began to hack it in pieces. They were in a blood frenzy paying no heed to the pain and anguish of their victim. By the time they were done the razor sharp instruments had hacked through her bones and left nothing but blood and flesh. A small pot was heated over a large fire and they dropped in pieces of her body. They were all engorged with bloodlust. Out of the fire of their offerings a horned beast appeared. His feet were like goats feet and he pranced about before them looking through to their blackened hearts. They were all ordered to use their small scimitars and make slits into their own wrists draining their blood into the pot. One of their members blacked out with horror and the creature took his body and tore it asunder heaving it to the side as if it were a sack of rags. Following the large creature were dozens of smaller ones. They approached each of the novitiates and, as vapors of smoke entered each one, the boys signed their names in blood. Moussaud remembered the pain at which his guiding spirit Rothar entered him seemingly tearing him apart and burning his heart with a searing scorching heat beyond the threshold of tolerable pain. The suggestions that were placed in his head by the creature were etched indelibly. There was to be no battle of wills when Moussaud was commanded to carry out orders that repulsed him such as maiming and torturing children, skinning people alive, cutting open victims and filling their body cavities with insects and snakes while they looked on in horror, Moussaud found himself compelled to obey the suggestions of his spirit guide. There had only been one time Moussaud had been able to disobey Rothar. He had refused to torment a young Israeli spy sent by the Israeli secret service to check the strength of Iran's anti-aircraft missiles. She had refused to disclose what she had learned while on assignment and was brought to the Black Flag for questioning. She was beautiful beyond anyone Moussaud had ever seen. Dark raven hair, well proportioned features, and eyes as blue as the Mediterranean Sea captivated Moussaud's heart. They brought her to their cave where they strapped her to the altar and Moussaud was singled out to torture her using live wires of electricity tied to a hand generator taped all over her beaten body. Moussaud turned away when he saw the girl had bitten through her tongue and severed it in half. He refused to cut open her stomach and fill it with live scorpions. He went up to her looked her in the eyes seeing her begging for death and slit her throat bringing her instantaneous relief from their hideous tortures. Rothar and the other spirits were furious because the girl was a Messianic Jew, one that believed Yeshua Ha'Meshiah or Jesus Christ was the Son Of God and died for her sins. She was immediately taken into the arms of a powerful angel and whisked away to heaven leaving behind her lifeless corpse which the group quickly hacked into pieces. Moussaud was lucky to escape with his life, their wrath was so great, yet unseen to him, a large powerful being, the same one that had directed his heart to one act of mercy, had escorted him out and away from their clutches.

After trailing them back to their hotel, Moussaud looked out of his car onto the Ethiopian countryside. He wondered how so many people could live on so little. With almost no farming land, poor running water and low food supplies he was amazed that Ethiopia could still support such a large growing population. He picked up his phone to call the Minister of Culture Ethiomu Hagid.

"Good Morning Mr. Hagid. I understand that a Ben Gibron from Israel contacted you about an exchange involving the Ark of the Covenant."

Ethiomu, a member of the Coptic Church knew that Moussaud

worked closely with the Arab alliance. He knew nothing about his Black Flag connections or that he was on the payroll of Prince Farshad. Still, a voice inside of him cautioned him to be very sparse with any forthcoming information.

"We have a lot of requests from people to see the Ark in Asmar. The requests are very rarely granted. No one sees it but the priest who protects it with his life and when he dies another protects it."

Moussaud was unhappy with his vagueness in answering and tried to draw him out a bit more. "I'm aware of that, but sources tell me that your government is planning an exchange of cultural artifacts, that you have contacted the Israeli's about getting back some original document from the court of Sheba. I represent a party that does not want to see this artifact fall into the hands of the Israeli's. It would only aid them in rebuilding the Temple and as you know that is the site of the most holy Dome of the Rock, a Mosque second only in holiness to my people to Mecca."

"I can assure you, my office is aware of no inquiries to this sort. We have no intention of letting the Ark or any other artifact go. We are not Egyptians. We are Ethiopians. We treasure our heritage."

In truth, Ethiopia boasted of the longest succession of royalty in the known world vaguely continuing for over two thousand years until Haile Selassie was deposed in the sixties bringing an end to a dynasty that repelled rule by outsiders for generations, only being subjugated by the Italians in the thirties. The Ethiopians were both a proud and fierce people, Ethiomu was proud of his heritage and knew that many of their current economic and social problems were the result of the years the country had suffered in the hands of Russian backed communists. He already saw the improvement now that the church had members in the government's circle of power.

"Mr. Moussaud. I suggest to you your sources are wrong. Please excuse me. I must go to an appointment."

Ethiomu walked down the hall to the office of the State Police to visit with Gerum Jama an old college friend who had risen to the rank of State director of Internal Security. He knocked and saw that Gerum was not in. He made a mental note to follow up the conversation. He had his doubts whether the Ark that was being protected by the Coptic Church was the real thing. Still most of the people in the church thought it was and worshiped it as if it were. Whenever it was brought out for public procession, the lines to see it were beyond what the eye could see. He stepped out into the street. He had grown callous to the needs of the homeless children more numerous than even locusts were. He could feel the money thick in his wallet but too heavy for him to lift out and share. Besides his reasonable salary as minister, he had considerable revenue coming in from the family coffee plantation high in the mountains. It was a large and prosperous business. The faces came to him begging for money, for food.

He looked at them with contempt. Tattered clothing, barefoot, shirtless, bodies thick with the dust of the street, eyes bulging out and shoulders narrow from malnutrition, they were as walking dead. He looked right through them and pushed them out of his way as he made his way to his Mercedes sedan. He didn't want to be late for the Insuee Club where he would indulge in the pleasures of the flesh.

He paid no attention to the statistics gathered by the United Nations Medical teams - that forty percent of the prostitutes were HIV-positive. He was driven by a force far greater than reason. It was no longer just an occasional sexual relief, it was a compulsion that gnawed within him and gave him no relief. He was always on the prowl and was on a first name basis with nearly every prostitute in Addis Ababa. He had been infected with Herpes, Gonorrhea, Syphilis, Hepatitis and had managed to keep all his various diseases under check. He suspected that he was probably carrying the AIDS virus when their newborn child died less than three days after birth. The infant was born blind with external lesions. Ethiomu had looked upon him like he was an alien. Before his wife even awoke from the anaesthesia he had the child removed and sent to nursery where it spent it's entire three days on earth in utter loneliness and ravaging pain. Devoid of human contact and eaten by the various viruses passed onto it from the sins of its father, it died uncomforted and was unceremoniously cremated.

The image of his child's face haunted Ethiomu but he felt no regret. His heart was devoid of even paternal affection. He was so decayed and corrupted that nothing mattered. If he had been able to see his soul he would have seen the utter filth and recoiled in horror at what he had become. The intermingling he had done with the countless prostitutes had opened him up to a whole new world of the spirit, a world so dreadful it kept itself in the darkness where no one could see. Nearly fifty demons dwelt within him, each one propelling him on to more and more sexual encounters and continually demanding so much that he was never satisfied. His lusts burned like a fire that never had enough fuel and they had consumed all he was.

As he drove from the government center out towards the airport he watched the sun begin it's decent into the night sky. His conscience, though nearly dead, still replayed the image of his young son grotesquely deformed, screaming in pain. He shook it off and thought about the pleasures awaiting him.

Buto, one of his many sexual partners had seen one life tragedy after another. Her family was from Eritrea which had fought a long hard war for independence from Ethiopia. Her people were proud and resourceful and though outnumbered a hundred to one had managed to finally achieve their independence and statehood years earlier. For her, the costs were high. At eleven both her mother and father were lost when a Russian made missile destroyed their home in the mountains. Her father had been the Mayor of their town, but with his death and the death of so many others she was forced to take what belongings she could save out of the wreckage and head for a larger town. She had been spotted by a group of soldiers in a transport truck going to Addis Ababa. They had taken her in and used her sexually. At first she cried, wondering how pain could be so intense, then after the last one had used her and thrown an old blanket over her ripped clothes, she lay in shock as if her head had been pommelled. They laughed when she rolled into the street as they forced her out of the truck at the city limits. They threw her meager bag of belongings out after her, scattering them all over the dirt road. Her young body had not even reached puberty. She stumbled into a Lutheran run orphanage and stood in line for food which consisted of a bowl of watery gruel and a hard piece of moldy bread. She ate it hungrily and slept outside of the gates hoping not to be bitten by the packs of scavenging dogs.

After several nights of sleeping outside, one of the workers took pity on her and she was given a bed of her own inside. They were surprised she was so well educated and put her in charge of teaching the younger students. The director of the Orphanage, Klaus Heinrich invited her to live with him and take care of his flat. One night after four years of faithful service, he walked into her room drunk and got into bed next to her. Though not as rough as the soldiers, he violated her just the same, bringing a further sense of shame into her heart. She ran away the very next morning and went back to living on the streets. She had grown into a tall shapely woman and eventually found it easier to sell her body which she despised and used the proceeds to sustain a meager existence. She knew she was infected with the AIDS virus and also knew there was no hope of cure. The sicker she got the more she hated those around her who weren't infected. She lashed out at those who were well and hoped they would die just like her in a steaming mass of viral decay. She didn't bother to tell any of her customers. She didn't care if they got it too. It served them right.

She looked out her window and saw Ethiomu knocking. He reminded her of several of the soldiers who had attacked her. She put on an artificial smile and opened the door.

"Ethiomu. Welcome. I wasn't expecting you so early."

"I couldn't wait. My visits with you are one of the highlights of my life" He noticed a Coptic Bible on her coffee table. "You read that?"

"Yea." Buto answered. "I'm going to die and I'm curious where I'm going to end up."

Ethiomu looked at her puzzled."We're all going to die sometime."

"I'm going to die soon." She dropped her top and he could see purple lesions on her chest. Skin cancer, AIDS. It is the final stage. before death. I can catch pneumonia, any bacterial or viral infection. My immune system is nearly depleted and soon I'll be at the mercy of all."

"That means..." Ethiomu stuttered

"That mean you have it as well. Didn't you just lose a child? You probably passed it on to him. You're going to die as well. the only difference is, we both know our deaths are imminent. We can't delude ourselves into thinking we will grow old and have plenty of time to prepare ourselves to meet our maker. Our appointments are soon. I'm just not so sure I'm ready to spend my eternity in Hell."

"I don't really believe in either a Heaven or a Hell. Why do you?" He questioned her.

"My life on earth has been too horrible to believe there won't be something better when I die and something worse to punish those who destroyed what God gave me without thought of consequence." Buto stated, pulling her shirt up to cover herself. "This Bible is quite literal in it's explanations. I'm just trying to find the escape clause. the words that will help me believe with all my heart that I can escape Hell and join my parents in Heaven. They were both strong believers as was I before they were taken from me."

Ethiomu who had taken off early in the afternoon to gratify his physical desires, desires which clouded out all sense of reason began to think clearly for the first time. He thought of himself as a mortal man standing on the threshold of a journey, a journey that he had not prepared for and not ever contemplated. He spent the next three hours talking with Buto and agreed to help her remain healthy and get her some government assistance, possibly put in a private sanitarium. He had seen the government hospices or hovels as they should have been named. Row after row of diseased women, men and children lying on the floors on old burlap sacks. Many were blind and mentally debilitated lying in their own feces, others with open sores on their faces, hands, genitals, with white blotches on their tongues and throats which made the simple act of breathing nearly impossible. The moans of those in pain and the lack of medicine and any type of organized treatment centers made the agonizing death from AIDS even more brutal. He was thankful for the handfuls of "Good Samaritan" organizations that had come in from various parts of the world to minister to those sick and dying. He knew they made a difference and he hoped he could get Buto placed with them so she wouldn't die as she had lived - alone and abandoned by all except those who wished to use her. He walked from her flat a different person. No longer lost and aimless, he was renewed with a mission - to find his eternal destiny. With the end of his life in view he was no longer able to look at the grim reaper and feign not seeing him. The knowledge of his impending death had brought him to the point where he knew he had to decide how to use his remaining precious days. He was like a man on death row, counting down his last hours, but it wasn't a last meal or cigarette he wished for, it was for a sense of purpose that would give definition to his short existence. He looked up to the hills surrounding the city and realized long after he was gone they would still be there. The guilt pangs of possibly infecting his wife hit him full force like a tropical storm shreds the beautiful swaying palms. He thought of her dying, their two young daughters left alone. In a country that had so many abandoned children that most people thought of them as less than human and cared for their pets with more compassion.

He decided it would be best to wait to tell her of his discovery until he knew for sure. There was never a good time to tell bad

The Voice

news.

***

He needed to get a fresh look at what it was really like for the people with AIDS. He had heard it was a slow torturous death but had never had the courage to see it first hand. Death was not something to be studied. It was something to be ignored. When someone died, the body was quickly buried and those who remained did so by pretending life went on as usual. He knew that the Lutherans were running an old hospital fairly close to where he was and he decided to pay them a visit.

Dusk had settled and the sky around him was a strange cast of orange, red and purple. The creator had spared no pigment in saying goodnight to the inhabitants of Ethiopia. It was a sunset beyond what he had ever seen in beauty and intensity. There were a few clouds on the horizon that looked like billows of flame. Outside the hospital was a tall wrought iron fence in need of painting. Gathered around were quite a few children, homeless and destitute. He wondered if they had parents inside. As he pulled up to the gate a short man in a security uniform saw his Mercedes and waved him through figuring him to be a man of importance.

Ethiomu parked and walked into the front lobby. Sitting in front of him were two young looking men. He could tell they were both blind. One had purple lesions all over his face. The other was pushing his wheelchair and when Ethiomu looked closely he could see his skin was ulcerated with open sores nearly covering his entire arm. He had white warts covering his face and hands and legs that stuck out from under his hospital gown. As he was transfixed staring at them he was approached unawares by a tall blonde German nurse.

"May I help you? Are you looking for someone?" She asked.

"I was wondering." He asked." Is there any hope? Does anyone survive?"

"Most die." The nurse replied. "We do our best to alleviate their suffering."

The Voice

"The man in the wheelchair. He's covered with warts and open sores. What does he have?"

"He's got atopic dermatitis, seborrheic dermatitis, sporotrichosis, and various bacterial and fungal infections."

"Can't you treat all the skin diseases, those things are mostly curable Aren't they?"

"Yes. In people without HIV they are but these people are immune-suppressed. They have no resistance to even the simplest disease, bacteria, viruses and fungus. Sometimes we can give them cortisone creams, but these are persistent infections. Those that you see there are just the external ones. The virus takes over the entire body." She pointed to a man sitting in a chair." That man was professor of Mathematics at Addis Ababa University, a PhD. Now he doesn't even know his name. The virus attacked his brain. He suffers from dementia. This disease is a killer. The people of your country have never taken it seriously. In central Africa there are entire towns wiped off the map, no survivors at all. That's why we are here to try and save your country."

"Is there any hope for cure? Vaccinations?" Ethiomu asked throwing out a straw. "Surely scientists have developed something to combat it!"

"We've trusted science for so long. We forget that science only works when dealing with known variables. There are many forms of the AIDS virus. They constantly mutate, and duplicate with extreme frequency. By the time you have learned how to manage one, it has already changed. This virus has a will of it's own. It has a mission of it's own, diabolical in nature. It's mission is to multiply and it doesn't care if it sacrifices the life of it's own host organism." The nurse replied.

"Don't you worry about catching it?" Ethiomu questioned. "After all everyday you are surrounded by it."

"No, I trust the good Lord. It is he who has called me to minister to the sick and dying. I pray for them, get them ready for their eternal journey. After all we are all going to die. Death's a certainty. Life and death. No one lives forever. This disease just puts people in the position to really deal with the main issue - Where am I going when I die?"

"By the way Ethiomu." Bridgette asked. "Do you know?"

"Yea." Ethiomu smiled. " When I die, I'm going nowhere. Six feet under the ground just low enough so some archaeologist doesn't dig me up and claim me to be some prehistoric man. I can just see it now. My bones traveling around the world in some scientific freak show."

"You have a good sense of humor." Bridgette smiled. "I guess it must go with your job. Oh don't be surprised. I know who you are. I speak your language. Your secret's is safe with me. Before you leave I'd like to give you something. You're a member of the Coptic Church aren't you?"

"Yes." Ethiomu nodded. "I was anyway."

"Well." Bridgette pulled out a small pocket size Bible. I'd like you to have this. I think if you read it you'll find it fascinating to learn just how many people Jesus prayed for that were healed of all types of diseases."

"Incurable ones?" Ethiomu questioned looking around at his future habitation.

"Yes." Bridgette responded. "What is impossible to man is quite possible to God. He's not bound by our earthly laws. He can supersede them at any time He chooses. It is He who appoints our time of life and our time of death."

Bridgette walked over and took his hand. "Though you walk through the shadow of death, He will be with you."

CHAPTER THREE
Magical Mystery Tour

Moussaud Hadidsian stood outside the Central Venue Hotel smoking a cigarette. He was dressed down but that didn't prevent the street kids from coming up to him every few moments with their hands out for a handout. He knew Ben had ordered a car and driver but had made nothing known to anyone concerning the destination. He had been unsuccessful getting any further information about them from the government. He had heard rumors there was a government authorized swap of relics, the Ark in exchange for various documents that the Israeli's had acquired from private collectors and museums throughout the world. Moussaud was wondering whether or not there really was an Ark after all. He reassured himself. "Allah is the only true God and Mohammed is his prophet."

An older Toyota Land Cruiser came pulling up to the Hotel. Moussaud walked over.

"Is this the car for Benjamin Gibron?" He questioned the driver.

The driver nodded. "Yes I am working for Mr. Gibron. Are you going with us?"

"No." Moussaud responded pulling out some money. "We'll be using the car for several days and there is no need for you to come along. I've been instructed to pay you in full. Here, this is a small fortune."

The driver's eyes widened as he looked at the pile of money being shoved into his hand.

"But the car." The driver spoke." I must stay with the car."

"No." Moussaud spoke peeling off several more notes, more than enough to replace the entire vehicle several times over.

"The car is yours." The driver spoke putting the money in his pocket. "If I need another one, I will buy one."

"Julie." Ben knocked on her door." Come on, we're trying to get an early start."

"There's no hot water." Julie said. "How am I supposed to leave without taking a shower?"

"Don't worry." Ben jested. "You'll be sitting downwind."

"Very funny." Julie replied. "You're a real Milton Berle, the only thing lacking for you to be a comedian is a sense of humor. I'll be right out."

Julie looked at her room. Right next to the hotel were hovels that the natives lived in. Shacks poorer than she had seen anywhere in the states, made out of crude branches, old pieces of automobiles, cardboard, all tucked into the gullies. She wondered why the country was so cursed.

She wondered how the world would welcome the news that the Ten Commandments had been found. She hardly knew anyone who even took them seriously. For most people lying was a daily thing. Say anything to get what you want was the rule of the day and as far as not using the name of God in vain, she could hardly recall a film she had seen where it wasn't used constantly. Keeping the Sabbath day holy, there wasn't a person around that wouldn't try to make a buck on a Sunday or spend it doing whatever they pleased. She went down the list and wondered what type a world it would be if people had actually lived up to the Commandments that God thought were important enough to write them with His own hand.

To be able to scientifically prove the eternal hand of God or the Almighty voice of God existed would be monumental in causing people to see their own error and folly. She knew how far she had walked from ways that were pleasing to God. She thought about the scripture in the Book of Genesis that Moses had attributed to God "Each man did what was right in his own sight." It reminded her just how far everyone was away from living the lives God had destined for them.

Moussaud was standing next to the car as Ben came out.

"What happened to the other driver?" Ben questioned Moussaud.

"I am the new driver." Moussaud replied in English. "But not to worry. I know the roads well. I am not Ethiopian but my family has been here for many years."

Julie looked him over as he was putting their bags in the trunk. She pulled Ben to the side. "We're going to trust our lives to him." She whispered. "I don't want to judge by appearances but he seems evil."

"I don't know what happened to our other driver but if we want to get to Asmar we have no choice."

"Look." Doug approached them. "I don't know what you two lovebirds are talking about but I'd like to get going and get there before dark. Did you check to see if the driver is carrying extra petrol?"

Julie looked at him with an accusing look as if to challenge him for calling them lovebirds.

"Yea, Julie, lovebirds, all birds squabble - it's part of their mating rites."

"Very cute Doug, linking me up with your sister. What now, are you Cupid?" Ben commented.

"No, just perceptive. Is there extra petrol?"

"Yes three cans."

Moussaud got behind the wheel and pulled out into the street, the car was immediately surrounded by young homeless children. They were pounding on Moussaud's window indicating that they had nothing to eat. Julie was moved with compassion.

"Let's stop and buy them some food." She said to the others.

"It will just delay the trip." Ben pointed out. "Besides you can't possibly feed them all, there's too many."

"Julie," Doug jested." You're not Mother Teresa."

"No." Julie said. "I'm not, but I'm not Scrooge. Driver would you pull up at that bakery. I do have enough to buy them all some buns."

Julie got out of the car and waved her money in the air. All the children started smiling and raced into the bakery after her. The shopkeeper was aghast and tried to rush them out. Julie showed her fistful of dollars and pointed to the stacks of baked rolls behind the counter.

"I'd like to buy all your rolls." she said peeling off a hundred dollar bill. "Make sure each one of these gets a package of rolls."

The shopkeeper smiled and humbly bowed before her, happy that she was caring for the children in her country. Julie walked back out to the car, children were streaming from all over into the bakery. They were chattering and excited as if St. Nick himself had landed a sleigh on the roof. She opened the door and climbed back in to everyone's astonishment with a big smile on her face.

"All right." Julie said." I've done my part today to help stave off world hunger now let's go help stave off world ignorance."

Moussaud turned to look at Doug. "Your sister, something missing in her head?"

"No." Doug smiled proudly. "Something is different in her heart."

Julie couldn't see because Ben was looking out the window but she had brought a tear into his eye. The one act of kindness she had done changed his heart more towards God than any sermon she could have ever preached, or theory she could have proved. The Israeli's were a compassionate people but only with their own kind by and large. Julie had demonstrated to him that those in whom resided the love of Christ truly had a love of another kind.

"You're really different. Did you know that?" Ben questioned. "But now that you've been the Good Samaritan for the day. We've got to get to Asmar for our work."

CHAPTER FOUR
The Confrontation

Ethiomu coughed up blood, bent over their sink. It spewed up on his dress shirt and tie. His head felt as if someone had been pounding from the inside with a heavy hammer trying to get out. Nothing seemed to quell the pain. He squinted his eyes and rubbed his eyes sockets which were bursting with the pressure. It was unbearable. As he was clenched over, his wife Gooma, a strong tall woman, from Eritrea came up to him. She looked at the blood in the sink and the blood splattered over his clothing and she turned around in disgust.

33

The Voice

"You sick man." Gooma said." You whoring around with those young girls and you sick. You go, you've got AIDS sickness. Go from the house old man."

There wasn't a hint of compassion and Ethiomu knew it was useless to pretend he wasn't sick, many of his countrymen had died from AIDS, there was no hiding it from anyone. He stumbled back into the bedroom opened a large plastic suitcase and began to pack it with his clothing. His two daughters looked at him with horror and watched as he drug it down the hall. They both wanted to run to him but were held back by their mother. They looked at him with sheer terror in their eyes as one would glance at a condemned man on his way to his execution. He looked at them, the terror gripping his heart. He wondered if he'd ever see them again. It was hopeless. He had often wondered what someone with leprosy felt like, ostracized from society, and for the first time he really knew. His heart filled with dread as he closed the door behind him.

Ethiomu went to his office and tried to concentrate on some of the paperwork on the desk in front of him. Sheba, his secretary, came in wearing a big smile and a hot red dress to go with it, she was disappointed when he didn't seem to notice her.

"What's wrong boss man?" Sheba said, proudly displaying an award winning set of ivories. You don't like my new dress. I wore it just for you. You sick or something?"

"My wife threw me out." Ethiomu announced "My party's over. No more whoring around. I've got AIDS."

"What about me?" Sheba asked her skin turning a pale yellow from fright.

"You too probably. Mine's just beginning to show. I didn't even know it till I got a lesion on my tongue."

"You've got a message from Prince Farshad." She said, disgusted with him and herself for sleeping with him.

"Just one?" Ethiomu inquired.

"Yeah." She replied. "But from the way it sounded, I wouldn't put it off. When you get off the phone we'll both still be dying." She managed a wry smile and left the room.

As Moussaud drove along acting as if he were a subservient Arab driver, his eyes carefully studied the road for their planned ambush. He knew the disappearance of two Americans and one Israeli scientist would not be taken lightly by the international community. Anyone who witnessed the pickup at the hotel, distribution of food to the poor, would surely have their report to give to the police along with a good description of him and his accomplices.

The hillside was rocky and full of shrubs. Pedestrian traffic had slowed down to a bare trickle. Every once in a while they'd pass a poor farmer and his wife prodding a donkey along. Julie was fascinated and her eyes drank in the scenery. They kept their discussion to a minimum, not wanting to let their driver know more than was necessary. Ben had been on the road to Asmar several times and wondered why Moussaud was pulling off to the right up a particularly rocky section of road.

"You're going the wrong way." Ben said agitated pointing back to the left.

"No." Moussaud said." I'm taking a shorter route we save time."

"What's wrong Ben?" Julie questioned, picking up on his discomfort.

"I've been on this road a dozen times." Ben said. "This doesn't seem like the right way."

Overhead Ben heard the sound of a helicopter. He cranked down his window and looked up. Hovering above them was a sleek black helicopter. The driver was a distinctive Arab. Instantly Ben reacted. He took Moussaud's neck in between his arms and began to choke him.

"Grab the wheel Julie." He shouted as the car began to crash into the rock walls around it.

They seemed to sail through the air as the car traveling wildly out of control careened down the hillside into a ravine. They were all dazed.

Doug was moaning and Julie was battered from the impact. Ben had braced himself and was outside the car trying to pull everyone out into the cover. They had landed in a thick grove of trees and were afforded some cover from the helicopter.

"Julie." Ben said struggling." Can you move your legs?"

"Yeah." Julie responded." What's going on? Why the helicopter?"

"They probably want to kidnap us, make sure the Ark never leaves this country. What ever we do, we'd better get out of here."

A soldier with combat experience has an edge over everyone else when he's in a life threatening situation. His body and mind go into another mode, one where one's instinct takes over. Ben's instinct for survival was high. He checked Moussaud's body and found a small Uzi. Doug was moaning and still unconscious. Ben drug him away from the car and hid him with Julie in the undergrowth. He heard the helicopter stirring up the underbrush and figured whoever it was they must have landed. He knew they were coming for them. Live or die, there was no other choice in his mind.

Quentin Girard placed the helicopter down about six hundred yards from where the Land Cruiser careened off the road. He checked the ammunition clip in the Uzi and got out of the chopper. He cursed when he hit ground and wished he had worn better boots. Jack Owens stepped out from the other side.

"You going to kill them?" Jack said sarcastically knowing Quentin would do anything for money.

"If I have too." Quentin replied. "The prince doesn't care if they live or die. He just wants the Ark."

Quentin reached in his ankle holster and threw a small seven millimeter to Jack. "Watch the chopper. I'll take care of the others."

Ben crawled through the wash on his stomach, trailing a brush behind him, trying to disguise his path. He knew any half-decent tracker could tell from a hundred yards away where he'd been and

36

where he was going. He was hoping that whoever was in the chopper had more experience in the air than on the ground. He hoped he'd gotten Julie and Doug far enough from the wreck that they wouldn't be detected.

"Snap." He heard the sound of a breaking branch as Quentin slid down into the wash.

Ben rolled a little to the right to get a good look. Quentin was jogging up the wash only about seventy five yards away. The Uzi was still slung over his shoulder and he was making no attempt to cover up his approach. Ben decided to wait until he found the car and then go for the kill. Quentin reached the car and saw Moussaud's body pinned under the door. He leaned down and checked for any sign of a pulse and felt the steel ring on his forehead.

"Who are you?" Ben questioned. "What do you want with us?"

Quentin turned from Ben, forcing Ben to move with him, catching him off guard.

Before Ben could adjust his stance, Quentin reverse kicked him in the kneecaps bringing him to the ground. Ben rolled with the kick out of the way and got off several wild shots filling the tree next to Quentin's head full of bullets. Quentin brought the Uzi off his shoulder and leveled it at Ben. His inexperience with the weapon showed, it kicked into the air as he pulled the trigger and Ben, still on the move, rolled behind the Land Cruiser for cover. Ben stood and got off a clear shot hitting Quentin in the side tumbling him over. The Frenchman gasped for breath as the searing pain coursed through his nerves. Ben approached him, gun drawn, sights aimed at the Frenchman's head.

"I asked who you were." Ben said leveling the gun. "Move anything and it'll be your last movement."

Julie walked out of the grove and they both turned to look at her. The Frenchman turned his gun on her, but before he could even squeeze the trigger Ben pumped three bullets into his face. Julie's mouth dropped as she watched the Frenchman fall face first into the sand.

"Him or us." Ben said explaining. "That's war."

"Who are they? What did they want?"

"I'd assume it has something to do with the Ark. There can't be any other explanation."

"We'd better get Doug. I think he needs medical attention." Julie said." He's barely breathing. He's probably broken a few ribs."

Ben hoisted Doug up on his shoulder and carried him up the wash. He had the Uzi slung over his shoulder and after a few pointers made sure Julie knew how to use the handgun. The metallic instrument felt deadly in her hand, it's weight bore an ominous foreign testimony to her heart of the depravity of man killing man as she reflected back on the first recorded murder - Cain and Abel. She wondered how the Mighty One's purposes were accomplished amongst so much violence and dreaded to be part of it. She knew since man had first sinned blood had been spilt on the earth and would continue to be spilt until Christ had come to restore His kingdom. The rocks were cutting into her heels and she wished she had pried open the trunk to take out her hiking boots. Ben motioned to her to wait beside Doug's body as he went up to check out the helicopter.

Jack Owens was waiting nervously pacing back and forth by the chopper. He had heard the exchange of gunfire and was quite unsure what to do. he knew he wanted no part in the killing. He reached inside his vest pocket and took out a flask of vodka and decided it was as good a time as any to have a drink. The warm liquid felt good as he let it drain down his throat. He wished it could drain out the emptiness within him - memories, pains, griefs. He knew it couldn't. It was no elixir or magic potion, just something to make his sense of recollection foggier. The memories would still be there buried, but still alive tormenting him.

He heard the sound of Ben's boot scraping on the edge of the cliff and turned to see just a moment too late. Ben instinctively brought the butt of the Uzi up and clubbed him behind the ear. It was a brutal crunch and Ben thought he might have broken his skull. He reached behind his ear to check for pulse. There was only a faint one. He whistled for Julie.

Julie came up over the side of the wash and found Ben preparing the helicopter.

"What's up?"

"We've got some new transportation." Ben said." See these registration marks? They are Saudi, this chopper belongs to the royal family. These people are really financed. Someone way up there doesn't want us getting our hands on that Ark."

"How'd they find out?" Julie wondered.

"Who knows? They could have us on satellite surveillance right now. I've got to do some modifications or we're never getting out of here." Ben saw her reaction to the other body." He's not dead, not now anyway. How's your brother?"

"He's coming to."

"I'll get him. Don't take your eyes off that one until I get back. If he tries to get up, shoot him." Ben didn't even stick around for her answer.

Ben struggled with Doug, trying to be careful lifting him up, but it was about two hundred pounds of dead weight. Even for his strength it took everything he had to just keep from dragging him up. As he shifted him and pulled him up so Doug's body was pressed against his back with his arms over his shoulders, Doug moaned. Ben deduced that he probably had broken some ribs and wondered if he was bleeding internally. A thousand thoughts were going through his mind and he wished he had a commanding officer to tell him what to do. He knew whatever decision he made not only meant his life, but the other's as well.

"Julie!" He shouted panting." Open that back door would you?"

Julie looked at him for reassurance." Is he going to make it?"

"Time to pray." Ben responded." He's pretty banged up. I'd suspect some pretty bad internal injuries."

"Can you fly this?" Julie asked.

"Yea." Ben responded." But I can't just fly it anywhere. It's registered to the Saudi's and they're not going to think too highly of us killing a few of their pilots."

"But they were trying to kill us." Julie reasoned.

"I don't think they're going to ask questions first. We've got to pray that your brother hangs on long enough for us to get up to Asmar, and then get enough fuel to get out of here."

As Julie opened the back door, Ben turned, hearing the man on the ground's groan. First he thought of leaving the man to die, and then struck with a rare moment of compassion, he decided to leave him with a few canteens of water and food as well. He pulled Doug into the back and tried to stanch the bleeding. A thought flashed through his mind that Doug might not make it. He quickly dismissed it.

Ben took the controls and after a few shaky moments of whirling in circles managed to get airborne. He looked back at Julie holding her brother's head in between her arms and wondered what it was about her that sparked him so much. The love he was beginning to feel for her was almost too much for him to handle.

"Julie." Ben addressed her. "I don't know if we can get your brother any immediate medical attention. I hope with all that praying you've been doing, that someone's been listening to you."

"Thanks Ben." Julie said. "God hears me, but I've got to trust Him no matter what the answer is. That's the way it is. He's not some Divine butler in the sky doing whatever I want Him to do. He's God. Jehovah. The Mighty One. When we prove it scientifically, the world will have to listen."

"That's wishful thinking." Ben reflected." Some people will deny things no matter what. They can have the proof staring them in the face and they still won't admit it. I don't think people are going to come running to God just because we can prove there was an Ark of the Covenant. They've got to want to know God before they'll ever find Him."

The Voice

"You sound like you're becoming a believer." Julie smiled.

"I've always believed." Ben stated. "I mean I've always believed in God. I guess I just haven't known how to reach him. I mean, look around us. Someone had to make this earth. Space telescopes like the Hubbell are telling us this earth, this universe is only ten thousand years old. That means that what Moses wrote in the Genesis account is scientifically true as well. It's pretty amazing."

"You study astronomy too?" Julie said curiously." I didn't know."

"All pilots need to be familiar with the constellations, the stars are just like navigators on ships. When I grew up on the kibbutz we had an old telescope. One of our elders, Saul Oshmara, explained all the constellations to me. He told me, from the beginning of time God had placed the constellations in the heavens to show men how to find Him."

"Why didn't you become an astronomer?" Julie questioned." Why an archaeologist?"

"Our country is full of history. Everywhere there are ruins of cities - digs. I guess I couldn't escape. When I'm older, then maybe I'll study the stars. We've got a slim shot of getting out of this country. The Saudi's have heavy influence down here. Who knows what they've given the Ethiopian Airforce. They're probably scrambling planes right now to look for us."

"What are we going to do?" Julie said in slight panic.

"We've got to get as close to where we're going and either ditch or hide this helicopter."

"You're kidding, right? You want to try and hide this helicopter? Where?" Julie laughed. "Under a tree?"

"Wherever. Maybe we'll build a structure around it. Netting, camouflage. It doesn't have to be anything great. Just so long as the pilots can't see it or pick it up on their infrareds."

When Jack finally came to, he felt as if something had exploded in his skull. The lump was the size of a small golf ball, but the throbbing was so intense he felt like he wanted to gouge his eyes out just to relieve the pressure. He stumbled up and wondered what he had done with the helicopter. He couldn't remember how he had come to be lying in the middle of the desert by himself. Overhead he heard another helicopter hovering and he felt the coolness of the rushing air as it landed less than fifty feet from where he stood. Before they could get him he had blacked out again. He had been unconscious over four hours.

CHAPTER FIVE
The Weight Of The World

John Reinhold was out in his side yard, bent over, pulling some weeds. Off about fifty feet away, their two golden retrievers were engaged in a dog wrestling match biting each other's ears playfully and jumping on one another. A pain hit John almost as if a sharp jolt of electricity had coursed his nerves. He went over head first. The two dogs ran over wondering if their master was playing a game with them. They circled around him and went closer to sniff him to see what was wrong. Red, the oldest of the two, heard him moan and got excited worrying about his master's safety. He barked and ran around trying to nudge him up with his snout. Tallow joined in, her barking even more furious. He was gone into a deep unconsciousness, nothing seemed to make sense and the world was floating around. It was as if the only thing connecting him to the earth was a thin cord that was stretching even thinner. Around him the blackness seemed to grow more and more encompassing until the only light before him was as a lone star in a world of infinite blackness. His life and deeds began to pass before him. Everything he had done that was evil and against his conscience gripped him, like a droplet of hot steel it burned his heart with the pain of his accountability. He wished he had done things differently but he knew he was powerless to undo the evils he had committed. One by one the deeds began piling up, the thefts, lies, lusting, fits of rage and anger, covetousness, taking of God's name in vain, coarse jesting, improper use of personal wealth, the impact of all of it hit him as the responsibility for his decisions fell fully on him. He didn't know if he was dead or alive but he knew he still existed and he was going to have to face an immortal God to answer for each of his deeds.

As his body lay lifeless on the grass his two dogs grew more and more frantic. Tallow ran back to the house and began barking furiously, alarming his wife, who, upon seeing him lying in a heap, immediately called 911. She ran out to him with a blanket not knowing what else to do but pray for him. She saw his face turning an ashen gray as the life giving blood ceased to course its way through his veins, the oxygen no longer pumping into his body. She knew they had very little time to try and save him or he'd be lost to her forever. The finality of death seemed so severe and she wished her daughter was around and could pray. It was funny how she knew her daughter's prayers were heard, and in her heart she cried out for Julie and her God to intervene and save the one person on earth she loved most, her husband.

As John approached the light it grew before him and he saw himself ushered into a large hall. He looked down and he was naked in a different type of body, but it was definitely him. The light coming from the Being on the throne was painful. It seemed to permeate every cell on his spirit body. It stung him to the quick. The pain was so real and yet was different from any earthly pain he had experienced. It startled his conscience with a guilt of his own sinful condition. He bowed before the figure and began to weep knowing that he was unworthy.

"You stand before me guilty of your sinful deeds, unwilling to turn from them and ask forgiveness. Yet your daughter has continually pleaded for your soul. So I have brought you here so you would see for yourself why you can't stand before me naked." The voice spoke.

The Voice

"What is it you wish me to do?" John trembled, his voice shaking in fear. "Am I dead?"

"No, to those on earth you seem dead but I have given you new years only you must use them differently. I have given you a new chance to serve me that your life may be redeemed from the vanity of living you have chosen thus far. Your preoccupation with material possessions, position, man's opinions, those things you previously placed importance on, will now vanish. You have seen the world that lies beyond and though when you return you will be able to remember only a little, that little will change your life. You must not try and stand relying on what you have done but you must know that Jesus has made a covering for you so your sinful deeds will not accuse you, and when you stand before me in judgment for your life you will be no longer naked but covered in a garment of righteousness."

John felt a hand pushing on his chest and started coughing. The paramedic who was giving him mouth to mouth was taken aback by surprise when he found himself breathing into the mouth of a live person. The light in the sky seemed golden as John tried to remember what he was dreaming. He couldn't figure out what was happening to him.

"John, John." his wife spoke. "You're back."

"Back." John said puzzled." I haven't been anywhere."

"You were lying here in the yard. You quit breathing. I thought you were gone. I can't believe it. I thought we'd lost you. But now you're here."

"I can't explain what happened to me." John replied. "But I know everything's going to be different. I remember I was talking to someone and He knew Julie. We need to get hold of her. I don't quite know what is going on but something is happening with her. I think I was up in Heaven, I just don't remember much about it except it was so beautiful. I've really got to change the way I've been living."

The Saudi Prince was furious when Jack gave his report of

what he thought happened. He had lost two good men, a helicopter, and hadn't the faintest idea of where the perpetrators were.

"Your majesty." Jack explained, sitting in a room overlooking the city of Addis Ababa. Below, the streets were teaming with poverty. "I don't know where they went. I heard shots and then the crack on my skull. I can't even describe what they looked like. But whoever stole the helicopter must have had considerable military training. You can't just turn the thing on and take off."

The Saudi Prince studied him. "I've already arranged for another helicopter to be flown here from Saudi. It's a fully equipped rotorless Apache. I hope you're up to it."

Jack was in awe."It might take me a little time to get acquainted with it but who's going to be the navigator."

"I will." Prince answered.

"Excuse me your majesty." Jack answered. "Did I hear you correctly?"

"Yes. You heard me correctly." The prince replied. I have full instrument training on an Apache. Everyone in the royal family was trained by the United States Airforce. I chose the Apaches, my brothers chose the F-15's. I wanted to be different. In this case that difference will serve us well. "

"So you can fly it as well?" Jack continued his questioning.

"Yes I can fly it." The prince replied. "But it is you who are the pilot. I will man the arms system, and blow this Israeli swine and his American accomplices out of the air. Disintegrate them. The only catch is, we must find them first. Get yourself cleaned up and something to eat. The helicopter will be here shortly. Time is of the essence. They could remove the Ark."

"What's so precious about the Ark." Jack questioned. "Isn't it just an archaeological treasure. It surely has no power of it's own."

"The greatest power in the world." The Prince answered. " The power of superstition, belief in an object, that alone can separate one people from another. Invincibility. Once they have their precious Ark the next thing the Jews will be talking about is rebuilding their Temple."

"What's wrong with that? Everybody's got to have their own religion. Why can't they live independently." Jack was uneasy with the change in mood coming over the royal prince.

"There is only one true religion and one God - Allah and Mohammed is His prophet. Until the world believes, all who do not follow Mohammed are infidels. Jerusalem is also holy to my people. Our Mosque rests on the site of what used to be the Jewish Temple, destroyed by the Romans in seventy AD. I know that you were raised a Christian but Christ was only one of many prophets, the greatest of the prophets was Mohammed. Look at your Christian country, flooded with pornography, violence, thievery, rape. Exporting to the world such unimaginable filth that the very planes from your decadent countries have to be checked when they land at our Saudi airports. Is this the legacy that your following of Christ has brought you to?"

The conversation was over, Jack was at a loss for words. He had been raised to believe in Christmas, Easter, the birth and resurrection of Christ but he didn't see how it had at all affected his life. He read pornography, loved violence and lived pretty much saturated by evil. He thought back to the Vietcong that had plunged to death from the helicopters, cruelly thrown to their deaths by pilots and aviators who relished in the inhumanity and realized that Christianity hadn't done anything at all for most Americans.

"We are corrupt. But it is because we have the freedom to be corrupt. In our country we don't legislate morals. What is right is not considered right for everyone. If someone wishes to purchase movies and videos with pornography they can do so." Jack added knowing that it was a hollow argument.

"I have met the young women who have been in your videos and magazines. Although, I have not indulged myself with them, many others of my family have hired them for parties and for entertainment. They are morally destitute. They will do unimaginable things for money. The women in my country are not corrupt like that. They won't even show their faces in public. Look at the disease that's killing the western world - AIDS. You don't find AIDS in my country. We are not cursed as you are cursed. This Ark represents to the Western world a return of power to Israel. I am sworn to stop it at all costs. This voice must not speak from the grave. Moses is dead. It is best it remains undiscovered." The Prince was livid.

"If we get it from the Israelite and the Americans what will you do with it? Suppose it was the dwelling place of their God?" Jack was probing to find out what he had gotten himself into. Was he unwittingly fighting against the creator of the universe the very creator that had led millions of people out of captivity and kept them alive for forty years in the desert? The one who had entrusted to Moses the Ten Commandments? "How can you wish to destroy such an archaeological treasure?"

"No. I do not wish to destroy it." The prince answered hotly. "But I will not allow it to return to Jerusalem where they can put it on display before the world. If I am forced to destroy it to keep it from going back, then I shall. There is only one God. He dwells not in an Ark but in the lives and thoughts of his followers. Surely even your religion has taught you that. Now let's take some nourishment. It won't be long before the hunter stalks his prey."

Ezra Davidnov was a first generation Israelite, his father Bensabid was a survivor of the camp of Buchenwald, one of only three thousand who had walked out alive. Katrina Davidnov, his mother, was from a wealthy merchant family that had started hotels in Tel Aviv and opened a small cargo service that brought goods back and forth by plane to Europe. Ezra was also the best friend to Ben. He was wondering why Ben hadn't made his usual afternoon call and was beginning to grow alarmed. He had a few connections with the Israeli space program and decided to check and see if their satellite over Africa could pick up anything unusual that could give him information as to Ben's whereabouts.

"Colonel Yassir." Ezra spoke firmly. "This is Ezra Davidnov.

I've got a problem. Ben hasn't checked in."

"How long overdue is he?" The Colonel replied, trying to weigh the gravity of the situation.

"Six hours." Ezra answered." I'm not trying to sound like an alarmist but these calls are scheduled, so if anything has happened we can get aid to him right away. Can you get a visual over Ethiopia?"

"The satellite's not due over that area for another five hours. can you supply me with his last known co-ordinates?" The Colonel questioned, writing everything down.

"Yes," Ezra said, "But it's probably not where he was heading. He was on his way to Asmar to make the rendezvous. He told me the road he was going to take. I have a map of it. I don't know how detailed and to scale it is but it's a start. I'll fax it over to you. Look I'm not going to wait around. It's only six hours by plane. I'll fly one of our courier jets over."

"Then call me on your SAT phone when you arrive and I'll let you know what I find out on satellite. Good luck. The Saudi's are using the AWACS so you'd better fly at sea level otherwise you'll be blown to pieces."

Ezra threw a few pieces of clothing into his bag. He checked the clip on his machine gun, oiled and ready, and threw in a few thousand extra rounds of ammunition. He had a full arsenal. He was one of the top explosive experts the Israeli Army had. If he could get next to an enemy communication center satellite dish, he could wire and blow it up while he was miles away enjoying a pungent cup of coffee. He was at their small family-owned airport within minutes, screeching a cloud of dust up in his red Lamborgini.

"Mom." He said to an elderly lady who's petite size and gold jewelry belied her power. "You've got to get a plane I can fly to Ethiopia. I've got to leave now. Something's wrong with Ben. He hasn't called in."

His mom knew all about the mission to bring back the Ark and restore Solomon's temple to it's former greatness.

The Voice

"I wish you'd concentrate on our business as much as you help that Ben friend of yours on his quest, but if you need a plane, no problem. You're the only Davidnov, so please don't get yourself killed. You'll give me a heart attack then we'll both be dead." His mom smiled laughing at the irony of her joke.

"If I die and you die then what's the worry? But don't worry Mom. I'm not going to die. I'm just going to help our Ben do what is important. If we're ever going to be a great nation again, it'll have to be because our God is a great God. Our size and military might aren't going to help us. 'If God be for us then who shall be against us?"

"You're quoting the Torah to your mother, Ezra? Please show some respect to your elders. Your dear father, God bless him, he will be rolling in his grave. If you get in trouble, call. We have some friends still in the cabinet. A lot of people owe me favors and I'm not afraid to collect, especially if your safety is at stake."

Ezra leaned over and kissed his mother, noticing her eyes were growing moist. He lingered just an extra moment wondering himself if he'd ever see her again.

"I'll take care of myself, Mom. Maybe something just happened to Ben's radio and it's not serious but I'm bound by my word to watch for him."

"Just as it should be, Son." His mother replied, holding his cheeks in between her tiny hands. "A man is only as good as his word. So keep your word to me and come back to see our family name live on."

Julie looked around at the desolation, wondering how she'd ever decided to take up science for a career. Doug was barely alive and Julie knew if they didn't get medical attention for him, each minute he was getting closer and closer to the door of death. The air was dry and she could taste the sand in her mouth and feel its grittiness in her hair. She reached for a canteen and looked up to see Ben coming back from his rendezvous. ▬

"Don't drink too much." Ben stated. 'There'll be plenty of food and water where we're staying."

"Where's that?" Julie looked at him admiring his strength under fire. "Have you gotten any help for Doug?"

"There's an American missionary doctor with Mission of Mercy, they radioed him. He's coming right over."

"How far away is he?" Julie wondered out loud." Doug is getting real bad. He needs help."

"I don't know how long it will take him to get here." Ben pointed to a group of Ethiopians. "You go with them. They'll take care of you until I come back for you. Doug will be alright Julie. Right now I've got to do a better job of hiding this helicopter or we're not getting out of this country."

"Where are you going?" Julie was desperate, afraid to be without Ben's protection.

As if reading her mind, Ben took her firmly in his arms and soothed her worried mind. "Jules, you be strong. We're going to get out of here. I promise you. Most people only read these kind of stories. You are making history, not just reading it. Our God will deliver us by many or by few, it doesn't matter if the entire Saudi Air Force is after us, the Russians, whatever. I've seen it before. The will of the Lord will prevail. Now I'm not going to tempt the Lord by letting my helicopter sit here waiting to be blown up. I need to get it into a cave where aerial photography can't track it. The Saudi's have every type of tracking device money can buy and they know how to use them. We have to assume they are still after us. So, go with my friends here. They'll give you shelter. I'll be back for you soon."

Julie watched as Ben took off in the helicopter. The Ethiopians had fashioned a homemade stretcher out of long branches. They carried Doug down the hill into a sparsely covered ravine. They made their way along the wadi and came up upon a thatch hut village with a few dwellings made of stone. In the center of the village cattle were milling about by a hand hewn wooden trough, and a thin child nearly skeletal was leading a small herd of goats.

The Voice

Julie felt abandoned. She had attempted to do something great that would bring God recognition worldwide and now she was faced with her first real failure. There was no one to lash out at, so she directed her thoughts to God, wondering why in the midst of her desperation He had abandoned her. Her accusations made her feel bitter and unsure of herself, the quiet confidence that had told her everything would be alright was replaced with an anxiety so intense that everyone of her breaths filled her with dread. In the distance she heard the sound of a helicopter and looked on the horizon to see a gun ship approaching. Instinctively she ran into the first building motioning her pallet carriers to come with her. The chopper seemed to be on top of the building and she braced for gunfire but the chopper pulled up and headed further down towards the excavation site. Her thoughts drifted towards Ben. She had only been away from him for fifteen minutes and she was already longing for him.

"Girlfriend." She told herself. "Get a grip on your hormones."

She chastised herself for falling in love with someone who believed Jesus wasn't the Son of God but just a misunderstood Jewish prophet.

Ben was covering the helicopter with huge sheets of rolled corrugated tin when he heard the distinctive sound coming from miles away. He had wished he had a little more time. He was thankful for the rough terrain. His guide Rebu motioned him to follow and they disappeared down the steep mountain trail. He wished he'd brought water and dressed for the extreme heat. Around him in the forest he could feel the eyes watching him. He was the intruder in someone else's world. The fame and accolades that he had been working for seemed insignificant in comparison to the lives of Julie and Doug. He hoped the God she prayed to had heard her and had a plan to get them out. She had finally convinced him that Christ was the Messiah. He didn't know what he would do with the information. Truly believing and following would surely bring the world, as he knew it, crashing down, hopelessly destroyed.

He wasn't looking forward to being branded as a follower of Christ by his countrymen, the name under which so many of his countrymen's relative's had died, exterminated in the concentration camps. A million thoughts were going through his head, he tried to clear his mind and concentrate on getting back to Doug and Julie. Unconsciously he sent up a prayer to God and decided to include the name of Jesus. It felt like the right thing to do.

Prince Farshad, flying overhead through the rough terrain, was awaiting the SAT transmission. A computer analyst back in Saudi Arabia would translate the satellite data foot by foot in a high speed computer and try to pick up the location of the missing helicopter. The Prince wondered how clever the Israelite was. He felt his mind fogging out as another spirit seemed to loom within him. Hate poured from his heart and filled every crevice of his being. His face, dark and weathered from constant exposure to the desert sun, turned a deep red and he turned to look at Jack.

"Where are they?" He screamed. "Go down closer to the trees. They can't have gotten away. There." He pointed to a clearing where an old black truck was broken down and a few peasants were struggling to get their goats out so they could change the rear axle.

"That's it." He cried. Mistaken, he grasped the lever and shot off several hundred rounds tearing the peasants and their goats to shreds.

In the distance Ben heard the sound of gunfire, there was no mistaking the sound of Apache guns. He heard an explosion and wondered if his helicopter had been found out. He took a second to assimilate where he was and his guide pointed in the other direction and motioned him to move quickly.

"You hit a bunch of civilians." Jack said. "I think it's time to get another pilot. I quit. I didn't sign on for murdering, Prince. I don't care how much money you got. I'm out."

Jack began taking the helicopter out of the forest and heading back towards the base. The Prince was livid and struck him full force across his Adam's apple knocking the wind of him. The helicopter started to nosedive as Jack alternately struggled for breath and tried to keep it in control. The Prince tried to wrestle control of the chopper from him but with his last burst of energy, Jack brought a thermos of coffee out from between his legs and smashed him full force in the face, breaking the bridge of the Prince's nose. The Prince turned white with anger, his blood draining from the surface of his face. He responded with a crushing blow to Jack's windpipe. As Jack's brain began to slowly fog from lack of oxygen, he realized that he was going to die. He decided that there was no way the Prince would live either. He pushed the lever forward throwing the chopper into a dive into the side of a jagged peak. The Prince looked in horror at the rocks, knowing that nothing would save him. His black heart was gripped in terror as he realized that his life on earth was over and he hadn't the faintest idea of what to expect from the land of death. He never felt the impact. It was so sudden, and the shock stopped his heart before he ever hit the rocks.

The huge explosion was visible for miles. Julie looked up from the small village and wondered if it was their helicopter that had exploded. She offered up a prayer for Ben's safety and turned back to tend to her brother. Miles away in Saudi Arabia the satellite flashed information on the thermal energy coming from outside Asmar. It was automatically fed via another satellite directly to the receiver on the Prince's laptop transmitter, it correctly showed the locations of the hidden helicopter too late to be of any use.

Back at Andrews Air Force Base outside of Washington D.C. the explosion of the Prince's helicopter was also monitored. Most of the communist countries were routinely surveilled and Ethiopia, though no longer a practicing communist government, qualified for surveillance. The tracker Ralph Jensen reported the incident to his supervisor. They were able to get satellite footage of the helicopter right before it crashed. Although the Saudi's were unaware of it, all the Apaches sold to them had a slightly different shape undiscernible to the naked eye but easily discerned by computer. The program check showed the supervisor that the chopper was Saudi. He immediately took the report to the base commander to be reported to the Security Council.

Ben had no doubt that a miracle had occurred. He knew with the sophisticated equipment carried on the Apache it would have only been moments before they tracked him down. He bowed his head in reverence for his deliverance. His thoughts turned to Julie alone with her brother and he wondered how to get them out with the Ark.

"Ben." Rebu addressed him." We have hidden the Ark not too far from here. Do you want to take it back to the helicopter now?"

'The real Ark." Ben laughed. "You never told me you had definitely recovered the real one."

"Have you opened it?" Ben was curious.

"No." Rebu was superstitious. All his life he had paid homage to replicas of the Ark as each year the Coptics paraded them down before the masses.

"I have seen many, many of the replicas. There is no doubt in my mind that this one is real. Come, your friends will be safe. Let us get it before something else befalls us.

CHAPTER SIX
All That Glitters

Ben and Doug had studied at least five of the replicas. Those versed in Mosaic tradition had told him what to expect from the real Ark. He had seen replicas made from the information written in the scriptures. He had seen artifacts thousands of years old and examined them for corrosion patterns. He was ready for the real item. He looked over at Rebu and grinned at how fortune had led him to a villager who's dedication and cunning had led him to the real Ark.

The Voice

"How much farther Rebu?" Ben said panting.

Rebu whistled a sharp series of bird-like sounds. A response echoed back.

"Not very far boss." Rebu smiled.

"Who was that?" Ben questioned.

"Mori. My son."

Mori was only about twelve years old, but like his ancestor King David, he was very good with a slingshot. He was tall with a carved Semitic face and very sharp features. He was handsome to look at and possessed delicate hands, the hands of an artist or musician.

Many weeks before, Rebu and Mori were wandering in the hills outside their village and had come across a small cave, nearly hidden from view. It was near the dig that Ben and Doug had established, but had been revealed during a slight earth tremor. Mori was small enough to fit in the opening and had found a clay jar covered with dust. When they opened it they found scribbling on it they believed to be in Hebrew. They had later discovered it was written in ancient Sumaric, a script such as was no longer taught in the schools. Rebu had tried to preserve the parchment but without the ability to seal it from the air, it had quickly disintegrated, prompting them to search the cave again to see if they could find another one. They had worked at night away from the watchful eyes of the Coptic officials who would never have permitted such a discovery taking place. When Mori's shovel had hit a wooden box he knew he was on the right track. A subterranean chamber had been carved in the side of the hill. They had found the resting place of the Ark.

They had told no one. They preferred to wait until Ben and Doug returned and share their discovery with them. Mori had volunteered to watch the entrance and had been guarding it only leaving occasionally to get food. No one from the village questioned why he was gone so long. They were all aware of how he made a living. His long absences never had to be explained.

The Voice

The terrain was tough and Ben was irritated that Rebu seemed to be moving through the brambles without effort while he was struggling. His intense pride kept him pushing but it was wearing him out. Rebu noticed the fatigue.

"You want to stop." Rebu addressed him with respect.

"No." Ben grimaced putting on a fake smile. " It's not going to kill me. We're almost there right?"

"Just down that next hill. We are very close. It's hidden near the lake."

The papyrus rushes were heavy and Ben's feet had trouble pulling out of the marsh. Each step was like a giant suction cup. Rebu, nearly eighty pounds lighter, travelled rather swiftly anticipating the joy of seeing his son after a nearly one week's absence.

Mori had spotted them while they were still a bit off and had run to meet them.

Ben was startled when Mori came alongside them and instinctively began to reach for his gun.

"Mr. Gibron." Mori smiled. "Glad you make it back. I have been guarding the treasure chest. No one has come. We have it."

"Son." Rebu addressed him." We must keep even more secretive. The Saudi's don't want this artifact leaving. They will destroy it and anyone with it if they find it"

"We can take it up the Nile, father. No one will be looking for us travelling by river craft."

"We have no boat."

Mori took his short machete and cut off a papyrus.   "We will build one just like they used to do. I have built many, father, only now I will build one for my people that we may once again worship in our own temple."

"Yes, Mori." Ben said placing his hand on the boy's shoulder in admiration. "Our people do need a new Temple and if we need to float up the Nile we will do so, but it is not very fast so we will pray for a faster way."

The Voice

Ben was taken aback by the beauty of the Ark. He had no doubt it was real. Everything in his being attested to it's veracity. Though the presence of God was rumored to have left it years before, it was untarnished as if time could not decay even the residual dwelling of the Holy Creator of the world. The cherubim on top which faced each other, wings touching, were still as polished as the finest modern piece of gold jewelry. The acacia wood in the interior was free from mildew and looked freshly oiled. The manna which had fallen out of the sky in boxcar proportions resembled heated misshapen sugar cubes. The two stone tablets looked as if they'd just been quarried. The almond rod which had budded was without signs of age. The wood poles that were fashioned to transport it from one location to another were as straight as a redwood tree; not even splintered or cracked with age. It was the most incredible phenomena Ben had ever witnessed. He fell to his knees in awe wondering why God had chosen him to be the deliverer.

Inside him a voice he had not heard since he was a child spoke to him.

"Ben, my child." The voice said "Do not worship the Ark. My presence can be in you as it was in the Ark. If you seek me with all your heart, you will find me. For he who seeks me shall not be disappointed."

Ben found himself crying, the weight of his sinful life was too much for him. He was a Jew, the son of generations of chosen people and yet he believed more in science than in the God of the Scriptures. He marveled at how God could care for him when he was so undeserving of any love.

He had set out to find the Ark where God had dwelt in times past, hoping to make a name for himself in the field of archaeology. He had gotten far more than he had ever thought possible - the presence of God had come to him and helped him find a faith so real he knew he could never lose it. He had an unquenchable thirst to know God to live with Him as one. He knew he had to open his life to it and in doing so, he would be altered forever. A peace settled over him as he left the cave. He was clear in his intention to bring the Ark back to Israel and share his story with the everyone. He knew he would never use the discovery for his own personal benefit but rather to bring glory to the One who had worked a miracle for him.

Ezra flew low over the hills surrounding Asmar. It had taken him just three hours to fully check his instruments and arrive in Ethiopian air space. He had flown so low to the Red Sea the white cap's foam had misted the plane the entire way. It was the only way he could avoid the sophisticated Saudi and Egyptian radar. He hastily checked his fuel and wondered where he could land. He needed at least a thousand meters to put the craft safely on the ground. He knew the best he could do was to land and procure some type of land vehicle in which to search for his friend.

He spotted smoke coming from the side of the hill. He took a wide turn and swooped down lower and saw the remnants of a downed helicopter. Using code he radioed back to Israel the position. He went by again registering the image on his nose mounted digital camera. He was going to get some answers. He only hoped it wouldn't be what he didn't want to hear.

While Mori was busy cutting the papyrus making the watercraft, Ben and Rebu returned to the village to retrieve Doug and Julie. He didn't know he was moments too late. Doug had died right before the missionary doctor had been able to treat him. He had succumbed to a massive head injury and had he lived would have been severely brain damaged. Julie was in shock when Ben arrived in the village.

She spotted Ben and ran to him clutching him in a deathlike grip. He was unable to respond to her level of grief. He reached down and embraced her, allowing her to bury her sobs in his chest.

"Julie." Ben said soothingly. "It's alright. Doug's okay. I know he is. He's with God."

Julie looked up large tears etching down her cheeks.

"You really believe it Ben." She choked. "I mean you really believe that he is fine?"

"Yes." Ben said." Our God is not the God of the dead. He is the God of the living. Your brother is still alive. He is just with God in another place. He believed in Jesus so he's with Jesus. Julie please listen to me. A helicopter crashed, they were trying to kill us to prevent us from getting the Ark back to Israel. We've got to go. They'll bring others back looking for us."

"Are we going to take the helicopter?" Julie asked.

"No, I'm not sure, we may even need to go by boat. We'll never be able to refuel the helicopter and they'll be looking for us everywhere."

"Where are you going to get a boat?"

"The old way. Rebu's son Mori is building a craft now out of papyrus. We'll dress like natives and float up the Nile if we have too. We have the Ark. It's unbelievable I saw it. It's beautiful. God spoke to me. I heard His voice. Just like when He spoke to Moses."

Julie began to cheer up realizing that grief for her brother could be put off. There was no time for self pity. She had a mission to accomplish, Doug was dead, there was nothing she could do to bring him back.

"I'll start gathering up some food." She slipped her gold watch from her wrist. "This ought to buy us plenty."

"What about Doug's body?" She asked Ben.

"They'll give him a proper burial here and when we get back we can send for his body. He's not here anymore Julie." Ben looked up." He's there in heaven, smiling down on us right now."

"You're right. I'll have to call Dad and Mom soon and let them know what happened. I don't know how Dad's going to take it. He and Doug have been pretty close most of their lives."

Julie didn't have the faintest idea on how long the journey would take. The Barkar River was a treacherous waterway dotted with rapids, snakes, and hippos with jaws big enough to crush a man in two. And after they passed the last populated area in

59

Agordat, they would still have over a hundred more miles to go. It was an impossible journey, but Julie knew somehow God would be with them.

After not hearing from his children for several days, John Reinhold decided to call one of his friends in the Defense department to see if he could get any information from U.S. people in Ethiopia. Ford Motor Company had a manufacturing division that did many items for the national defense, from all-terrain vehicles to brake pads, and John had made several contacts with the government through the years.

Robert Sweeney was in a meeting when John called and had to return the call. After a brief getting reacquainted chat, the talk turned to John's children in Ethiopia and Robert wondered what they were doing down there.

"They're trying to get the original Ark and return it to Jerusalem for temple sacrifice. They went with an archaeologist from Jerusalem, Ben Gibron. My son's been going on digs with him for over a year and a half."

"You haven't heard from them in three days. Is that unusual?"

"Yes." John answered." They always stick to their plan and their plan was to call in every three days, no matter where they were or how expensive the call might be. I checked with their hotel in Addis Ababa and they checked out yesterday. This is the third day since they were supposed to call. Is there anything you can do for me?"

"I've got a contact with the station chief in Addis Ababa, works for the U.S. Embassy. Let me get a request over to him and see what's happening. Was this thing government sanctioned? I mean if this artifact is on Ethiopian soil I don't imagine the Ethiopians will be too thrilled to have it leave."

"There was some kind of swap going on for some of their national treasures. "

"Do you have any contacts there? Names of people that might have been in touch with them?"

"There was an Ethiomu fellow with some government branch there." John added. "They didn't leave me much information. I've got a number for Ben Gibron's parents in Tel Aviv, but I don't want to alarm them before I find out whether anything is wrong or not."

"Look John." Robert explained drawing himself up in his chair, gazing over the trees outside. "Ethiopia is not a real friend of America or Israel either. Just a short while back they were totally communist. So hold tight, it might take awhile to get some information."

"What's your friends name?" John asked.

"Wilbur Tonney." Robert said. 'He knows the country well and he's fluent in a half dozen languages plus he's got some good contacts with the Israelites."

After a little more small talk Robert hung up and made some calls. First he called over his secured line to Wilbur in Ethiopia and then he dialed a friend in the Department of Defense. He found out about the unidentified crash of a Saudi armed gun ship and knew somehow the incident had to be connected. It was rumored that Prince Farshad had not returned and was missing. It was no secret to anyone in the intelligence community that Farshad was violently anti-Semitic and despised his own ruling cousins who accommodated the Israelites. About three hours later Robert got a call back from Wilbur.

"I checked on that Name Ethiomu. His last name is Habran. He's the minister of Culture, it's rumored that he's dying of AIDS."

"Does he have any Saudi friends?" Robert asked.

"I was just getting to that part." Wilbur said. "We ran a check on his bank account and he just received a rather large transfer from a Saudi controlled account in Switzerland. So apparently he's selling them something."

"Or someone." Robert said." Have you got any news about the helicopter crash up by Asmar?"

"We just heard about it." Wilbur was impressed. "How'd you hear about it before me. I'm supposed to be the Station chief for crying out loud. A lot of Saudi's have just flown in, rumor is it might have had some high level family member in the gun ship. Whatever it is, it was never registered to fly in Ethiopian airspace it was a rogue acting independently of any official government sanction."

"Do me a favor Wilbur. A good friend of mine has two kids over there missing. See if you can get anything out of Ethiomu Habran."

"You think he might want to clear his conscience?" Wilbur asked.

"It's worth a shot." Robert said. "Look I'm going to owe you big time."

"You already do." Wilbur laughed. "But who's keeping track?"

Wilbur left the Embassy and stepped out into the Ethiopian haze. A city of ten million people with inadequate food, transportation and water. It was like living in a famine zone. Everywhere he looked there were hungry starving faces wondering why they were born into a world with so little to offer. Wilbur tried to keep a compassionate heart, but he had long ago given up on the idea that he could make a real difference. A young child ran up to him, its hands outstretched. He looked in its eyes. There was still a sparkle of hope that a random act of benevolence from a stranger could make a difference. Wilbur reached in his back pocket and pulled out a twenty dollar bill. He slipped it to the boy. The eyes lit up as the young boy realized the fortune that had been given to him. He hobbled to where his mom was resting on the street, gaunt and nearly starved. She lifted her emaciated frame and smiled at Wilbur. One at a time, he thought, and walked away.

He knocked on the door of the house of Ethiomu, a young girl answered. She was pretty with pigtails and a bright pink frilly dress.

"Is your father home?" Wilbur asked.

"No. My father's sick, he doesn't live here anymore." She replied.

Before he could get any more information out of her, a maid

came up to the door. She spoke in broken English.

"Mr. Habran no live here anytime. He very sick. He got the death." She slammed the door on him leaving Wilbur to wonder what she was talking about. He knew Ethiomu's reputation. It was his job knowing something about everyone. He decided to pay a visit to a well known call girl figuring he'd find out what he wanted.

He swung his Toyota into the rather heavy traffic. The bus in front of him, though small, had over twenty people sardined inside. Several were hanging halfway out the window. Branches sat on the top along with assorted sacks. Everywhere he looked, all he saw was hopelessness. He wondered about death and how he would die alone, no family, no wife. He wondered how he would answer to God for the lies he had routinely told in the course of his job. He wondered where he would spend his eternity. He looked down at his own stomach stretching out several inches over his belt and then looked at the women and children sitting on the sidewalk without an ounce of fat anywhere on their bodies, and wondered if he'd be judged for ignoring them. The street was full of potholes and he bounced up a rather steep path towards the club where the government officials went to spend time with their mistresses. He thought back on how he ruined his own marriage to Sally Ingram by bringing her home an infectious disease from Bangkok. He was still ashamed she had contracted cervical cancer and died within three years, never even suspecting the cause. He had lied about that as well, ignoring her complaints of pain to cover up his own indiscretions. His eyes grew moist and he hoped someday she'd forgive him. He hoped even more that God would, but wondered if he would ever forgive himself.

The Bombay club was run by a wealthy Indian man who had no qualms about recruiting young girls to be bar maids, sitting with patrons and taking them to back rooms to indulge their sexual appetites. Indar Katari didn't care who did what with who, he just wanted his cut. He sported a heavy gold necklace, alligator shoes and the finest watch money could buy. He had made a fortune, especially by Ethiopian standards. There was nothing that couldn't be bought at the Bombay club. The government left him alone. A private room in the back was well stocked with every imaginable scotch, champagne and wine. The music blared out old American disco hits and the club was decorated in red velour and black with pulsating lights. It was late afternoon and it was packed with foreign visitors and young nubile Ethiopian girls, bought from their parents and villages and fattened up to make them more appealing. The girls didn't even know the way they were living was wrong and went against God's commandment - not to commit adultery. They just knew they had a place to live and plenty to eat. Many of them took what money Indar allowed them to keep and sent it to their homes to keep their parents and brothers and sisters from starving.

As Wilbur entered he noticed a group from Saudi sitting at a private booth, he saw Ethiomu in the booth with them and had to take a second look. It was obvious the man was deathly ill. His face was distorted and had a large purple welt on it and he was coughing, rather hacking, as if he had a mouthful of phlegm. Wilbur edged up trying to get within hearing distance while not being obvious. He knocked over his drink and the waitress came scurrying over.

"You want another?" She asked him. "I can bring you a fresh one."

It was too late, Wilbur felt the eye of a dark skinned Saudi man bearing through him as if he were at the end of a laser beam on full power.

"Sure." He replied nonchalantly, appearing to ignore the conversation. " I think I'll move to another table."

He knew there was no chance to listen in and he decided to follow Ethiomu after the Saudis left.

The Prince's disappearance had created a furor in Jeddah. Several of his brothers had talked to the King and openly complained about Farshad's disappearance and rumored death and his quest to prevent the rebuilding of the Jewish temple. They had

The Voice

succeeded in convincing the King to mount a full search in Ethiopia.

The King had thrown his full weight behind the search to find his missing cousin and demanded that the Ethiopian Minister of Defense allow armed Saudi Aircraft to enter the Ethiopian airspace. They were not just interested in finding Farshad. They were interested in keeping the Ark from ever returning to Jerusalem where they were sure it would raise the national consciousness to such a fervor that the people would demand a new Temple that would threaten the Muslim's second most holy site- the Dome of the Rock.

Word travelled back quickly through the CIA and it wasn't long before Robert Sweeney got wind of it.

"John." he said. "I've got news out of Ethiopia. The Prince is rumored missing, presumed dead and his quest to have this Ark stopped from leaving Israel has been taken over by the old king himself."

"Any news of my son and daughter and their Jewish friend?" John was sweating and he tried to keep the salty liquid from stinging his eyes.

"No, not much, some rumors from our man in Addis Ababa. He finally spoke with the Minister of culture and found out that all along they were just using the Israeli team to flush out the Ark. They've never had any intention of letting it leave their country. The Saudi's have thrown a lot of money into Ethiopia; they pretty much get what they want done there. I've got some friends that do airlifts to some of the relief groups up in the northern part of the country. I'll give them a call and see what they've heard. And I'd do some praying. Rumor has it, the Ethiopians are going to allow Saudi aircraft over their territory and there's nothing the Saudi's haven't bought from us."

Ben stood next to Julie, the body of Doug wrapped in white sheets was laid out in the grave and Ben had his arm around her. Julie choking on her own tears knew she had to say something but she couldn't coordinate her mouth, she was convulsing too bad. Ben, misty, but having been hardened to the realities of war and death drew her closer to him and began his prayer.

"God. We know You are good and we know You've taken Doug out of this world into a better place. So I'm asking you, God, to see him safely on his journey and make a place for him in Heaven with You. Comfort Julie, help sustain her through this loss and don't let this death be in vain. Use the discovery of the Ark for Your glory that the world might see that there was a God in Israel that still rules the universe."

Julie was holding a bouquet of flowers handpicked from the valley. She threw them on top of the body and wept.

"Goodbye my brother. I loved you and I'll miss you. Rest in peace. I'll see you someday in Heaven. Watch us as we make our journey back home. You didn't lead a long life but I'm proud of you and I'm sure Mom and Dad are as well."

Ben had to pull Julie back from the grave, she was shaking so badly, he didn't want her to fall in.

"Come on Julie." Ben said. "We need to get going."

Ben was unsure exactly how they were going to get through Sudan or whether they should risk going through the Red Sea. He knew it would take an act of God to get them back to Israel but he couldn't bring himself to share his uncertainties with anyone else. It was on his back and even if the load was going to break him he was determined to bear it alone.

He snuck a sideways glance at Julie. She was eating some wat with the Engedi sponge bread. He marveled at how quickly she had come to terms with her situation. He'd met a lot of girls like her in Israel. He'd served in the armed forces with them but no one like her since he'd been out of the army. Her will to succeed was contagious. They both knew that if they didn't return with the Ark that Doug had died in vain. He looked over the map studying all the possible escape routes. He decided that a trip through Eritrea would be best and figured if their luck held out he could possibly catch a boat out of Massawa that they could engage to at least get them up to the Sinai.

"Julie, don't pack too many fresh foods, take mostly biscuits and a few jugs of water. It's going to be almost five days by boat to get to Massawa, So don't take things that are just going to spoil."

"Okay" She replied. "Some of the women made us barley cakes and I've got a bunch of sugar cane juice for energy. Look, I found out there's a phone not too far away. I'm calling my dad to let him know where we are."

"If anyone sees you." Ben hesitated. He knew she had to tell her parents about Doug. "Look, just make sure nobody sees you. Cover yourself up, veil your face and don't be down there too long."

"What should I tell my dad?" She questioned.

"Tell him we're on the way to the harbor." Ben reached in and gave her a number. "Tell him to contact this number in Israel. If anyone can get us out, Ezra can."

Several of the village women lent clothing to Julie and within minutes she looked like a typical Moslem women, nothing showing except her eyes. A young girl, Tirra, with cornrows in her hair and large earrings was to guide her back and forth to town. Julie wished she knew more Amaharic. She was unsure whether or not the local phone exchange would be able to get her in touch with an international operator.

They climbed out of the small valley and looked at Aksum, not a large city, but one dotted with small thatch-like houses and a few brick buildings alongside of the main Coptic Temple. Julie felt a pang of guilt for helping remove their most sacred treasure but knew God had led them to it and was honored that He had chosen to unveil it during her lifetime. She felt weightless. Something was happening inside of her. She had never felt the depth of emotion that she felt for Ben. There was no way she could even register how he made her feel. She knew the odds were stacked against them in returning to Israel, but she felt confidence in Ben's ability to get her there safely. As she walked down the path she wondered about how life would have been if she had been born a Moslem. Born, believing in Mohammed, into a culture where women were treated as chattel - in no way equivalent to men. She was grateful for being born into a country where there was respect for women and even more grateful for having the opportunity to hear about the saving grace of Jesus Christ and having been able to experience his forgiveness.

Underneath her feet she could feel the hard rock of the mountains. The ground was unsteady and several times she struggled to keep her footing. She wondered why, in a country where so many were on foot, so few owned any decent shoes. She thought of her closet and how she had shoes for every occasion and every sport and how they made do with just one pair of poorly made sandals. The sun was setting and making it harder and harder for her to see. She could hear the screeching of nearby baboons and wondered if they would challenge her passage through their territory.

The town square was clogged with Daitatzu transports, they were miniature in size and held a disproportional amount of people. Each one seemed to have at least fifteen or twenty people with everything from bags of coffee, goats, chickens, and bolts of cloth piled high on the roof. No one paid her much mind as she went to the Ministry of Communication to make her call. She never noticed the man standing across wearing dark wayfarer style sunglasses smoking a cigarette. Khan Abdu Seid had a trained eye and the minute he saw the way Julie was walking he knew she was an American. She was much too assured of herself and walked with far too much grace to be a Moslem woman. He threw down his cigarette and followed her in. He watched her fumble with her small cloth coin purse and hand the lady money for a phone call. It was obvious she was unacquainted with Amaharic. He smiled and wondered how his director knew enough to plant a lookout in Asmar. His skills in English were not good enough to allow him to hear what she was talking about, but he knew she was the one he was to have found and he smiled at the thought of the fat reward coming his way.

CHAPTER SEVEN
Angels All Around

"Mom." Julie exclaimed wondering why her own voice was continually repeating itself, not understanding the echo on overseas calls.

"Julie is that you?" Her mom answered. "How is Doug? Your father and I are so worried about you. You agreed to call us. Where have you been? We called your hotel and the American Embassy. Your father even got hold of some government friends. Your father's not here."

"Mom." Julie thought and decided not to withhold the bad news. "Doug's not coming back. There was an accident and he's in Heaven."

Julie could hear the silence and the deep sobs coming from the very bosom of her mother, a women protected from so much sorrow who would certainly be changed forever by the death of her only son.

"Mom," Julie said." I only have enough money for three minutes. Take this number and call Ben's friend Ezra. We are being followed. Tell him we're outside of Aksum and we're going to be in Massawa in about five days in the harbor. He's got to try and pick us up there. We found the Ark, Mom. Doug didn't die in vain. I love you Mom. I'm sorry to tell you such horrible news but he's with Jesus. Everything is going to be okay."

Julie decided to take advantage of the trip into town to pick up some additional supplies for the trip up the river. She wasn't the slightest bit cognizant that she was being followed. She wandered into a pharmacy. The lack of supplies available shocked her but she picked up some quinine for malaria and some aspirin. She wished she had known the language better and could have asked for water purifiers. She thought back to the Bible where it said. 'If you drink any deadly thing it shall not harm you', and sent up a silent prayer. She knew that God was good and would take care of her. She caught a glimpse of a Middle Eastern man coming into the store as he passed her she noticed a glimpse of blue steel under his jacket. Her heart began to race. As she stepped out she looked for the woman who had accompanied her to the city. She was nowhere to be found. A Mercedes limo pulled up in front of the drugstore. The windows were heavily tinted and there was a small flag where the antenna should have been. She didn't recognize the pattern and couldn't identify the country. She tried to get around it and out of the corner of her eye saw the rear door open and two men, smaller in height than her, race towards her. She wished she hadn't dressed in such cumbersome clothing. She tried to run but only got about ten steps. All around her people turned the other way. She felt her arm pulled back almost to the point where her elbow joint was breaking.

"Get in the car calmly." The man spoke, his steely blue eyes looking at her. "If you don't come peacefully, you'll never use this arm again."

She gave up her struggle and submitted. Her chest felt as if someone had placed it in a glacier spring. She began to shiver quite involuntary knowing that whoever it was that was after the Ark had made her an integral part of the game. They hauled her between them into the rear seat. The man who had wandered into the pharmacy came out chewing a chocolate bar and got into the front seat. Four to one, she knew the odds of beating them were insurmountable. She would have to pray for some way to escape.

The man in the front seat wasted no time. He turned around and ripped off her turban and veil. When he saw her face he smiled and commented to his friends in Farsi. They all laughed. She assumed it was at her expense.

The Voice

"We are from the People's Revolutionary Party in Iran. Our brothers in Arabia have asked us to help them get back a valuable religious relic which we have information you are intending to take back to Israel. You can tell us where it is and we'll put you on a plane and send you back to America, or you can make it very unpleasant for yourself."

"I don't know what you are talking about."Julie said trying to muster as much conviction as she could in her shaky voice. "I'm here as a student writing a thesis on the difference between Moslem women and Western women."

"Where is your friend the archaeologist Ben Gibron." He produced a picture of her and Ben outside of their hotel in Addis Ababa.

"He's not my friend." Julie spoke. " He is a friend of my brother. I'm just up here hoping to find them myself. They left our hotel several days ago and said they were coming up here. I haven't heard from either of them and grew worried."

The man in the front seat grew restless. He didn't know whether or not to believe her. It would be a pity, he thought, to subject someone of such beauty to the tortures of his friends. She might be telling the truth. He didn't know.

The car pulled around the corner. There was an airport close by and she could see some small planes landing. She wondered where they were taking her.

"We can remove you from this country and you will never go home to see your family again. You will be a slave in some sheik's harem. It's not a very pleasant life for one used to such freedoms as your country affords you."

"I am telling you the truth." Julie said, hoping God would forgive her for lying, wondering if it was a lie to refuse to divulge information to a sworn enemy of his people. "From what I have been told all the religious relics are in the churches. I don't know what you want from me. Just because my brother and his friend are archaeologists, what does that have to do with me?"

The Voice

Ezra's plane had been undergoing standard maintenance work in Aksum. Ezra was supervising, making sure that everything was done strictly according to procedure. One slip up and he knew he would be hurled thousands of feet down to his death. He was doing the instrument check himself when he saw his light go on. He picked up the hand-held receiver and dialed in for a clearer reception.

"Come in. Come in Gideon's Trumpet. This is Mama Hen." He spoke in Hebrew.

"Lost travellers are down wind. Requesting pickup in Massawa five days." The operator told him.

"Mother Hen I read you." Ezra spoke." Where are they now?"

"Last contact Aksum sixteen forty, over. Call if you need assistance, Red Eagle standing by."

Ezra was glad for the code. He looked down at his watch and wondered how his mom had gotten the message so fast. He didn't know that less than a minute after Julie's mom had hung up the phone her father had come in and called his number in Israel. He stepped out of the plane just in time to see the black Mercedes pull onto the landing field. Down farther on the Tarmac a distinguishingly marked Boeing 737 was parked. He identified the markings as Saudi Arabian. A chill ran down his spine when he saw the rear door opened and a beautiful American woman in partial Moslem garb being pulled out. He watched the tallest man approach the ground manager and begin arguing. He couldn't hear what they were saying but assumed they were demanding the plane be cleared for takeoff. The Ethiopian ground manager was a tall Eritrean. He sensed that something was wrong, that the girl was being taken against her will. He was doing his best to try and thwart their leaving. The man followed the kidnapper and pointed to the fuel trucks gesturing wildly.

Ezra bribed the Ethiopian checking his plane for his ground uniform and went into his cockpit and took out his nine millimeter tucking it under the overalls. He worked his way over to the fuel truck keeping his head down so his Semitic features would not be recognized and began to help with the refueling. He was able to get a closer look at the girl and tried to make a signal to her with his eyes. Just as he was completing his signal Abdol turned around and noticed her looking at him. He grabbed her severely on the arm to chasten her for not being a cooperative hostage.

"We gave you a chance to cooperate. Now you are coming with us. In less than one hour you'll be back in Addis Ababa and what happens to you there rests entirely in your hands."

Julie didn't realize that such hatred was in her, but looked at him as if she could kill. It humored him to see her so mad.

"You are not such a meek dove are you." Abdol grinned. "You have spirit like a proud mare. Well, even the proudest of mares can be broken. Tell us, where is the Ark?"

Ezra was close enough to hear.

"I know nothing." She replied defiantly. If you wish to find the Ark, you must ask Ben Gibron himself. I have not seen him. Why are you wasting time with me? What interest would I have in a religious relic. I am a student. I am only interested in my studies. Whomever you work for will surely be displeased that you have wasted your time on one so insignificant."

Abdol looked at her not sure whether or not to believe her. She turned her eyes in the direction of Ezra who was raising his gun to shoot him. It was just enough warning for him to see what was coming and duck under the car. Ezra got off a wild shot and had to take cover behind the fuel truck. Julie took advantage of the confusion and ran towards her unknown rescuer. She found him crouched behind the fuel truck pinned down by the incessant machine gun fire of her former captors.

"Ezra." he said extending his hand. "I saw you being taken away. I figure you must be Doug's sister, right? How did they capture you?"

Julie nodded and replied. "I went into town for a phone call. They must have had lookouts posted to see if any of us would turn up with the Ark. Ben is still hiding in the valley. We were planning on floating down to Massawa in a homemade boat."

"First we need to get out of here. When I give the signal get in the fuel truck."Ezra stood and fired off several shots hitting one of the Moslems who were spraying everything with their automatic weapons. Ezra motioned and Julie jumped into the truck cab. Ezra piled in next to her and pulled out, ripping the fuel line from the plane and spilling fuel all over the ground. Ezra looked back and fired in the direction of the fuselage where the most fuel was spilled. The spark caught and set off an explosion. Ezra took Julie's arm and dove out of the fuel truck. She twisted her ankle as she hit, but he pulled her up and they headed towards the terminal. He watched from the window as the Saudi plane went up in flames. He saw the face of Abdol through the flames and wondered why it looked familiar.

Ezra wasted no time in getting Julie out of the airport. He was hoping no one recognized him and wanted to get enough distance away that he wouldn't be identified as the owner of the other plane. Outside the airport a maintenance truck was parked. The large crew was working on the landscaping and had left their keys in it. Ezra looked in the front window and not noticing anyone motioned Julie to get in.

"We're stealing this truck?" Julie questioned.

"That's right unless you are suddenly bulletproof."

She jumped in and they headed for the exit road. A lone guard was outside watching the Saudi plane ignite melting everything near and sending loud explosive sounds reverberating. Ezra put his head down and motioned for Julie to do the same. They crashed the wooden pole at about thirty five miles per hour, totaling their front windshield, spraying the inside of the cab with shards of safety glass. The security guard was too shocked to pay them much mind. They pulled out into the street and headed back towards town. Dilapidated fire rescue vehicles were heading towards the flames. One was no more than a converted water truck and the other was an ancient ambulance that looked like it had been left from the Italian invasion of the forties.

"You know how to get back to the village where Ben is?" Ezra questioned.

"Yea." Julie said, speaking before thinking. "I think if you head northwest of town we should find it. There isn't much of a road, we pretty much walked on a dirt tire track."

The road back was full of potholes and obstructed by several fallen trees and boulders. After about thirty minutes of driving and maneuvering, they pulled into the village. Julie glanced at a large group of villagers gathered together. Ezra honked and they moved aside. Mori was holding Tirra and some of the women were gathered around. She had a nasty gash on her forehead that one of the Iranians had delivered to her. No one could believe Julie was back and when she got out of the truck, they parted for her as if she were a ghost rising from the dead. She saw Ben and ran to him crying, he welcomed her with open arms.

Ben turned and looked at Ezra. "I'd never believe it. I owe you big time Ezra."

Ezra smiled. "I don't know what you've done to have gotten half the Saudi army on your case but whatever you stirred up I don't think we should stick around for the consequences. I just blew up one of their private jets and someone is not going to be too happy with me. We've got to get back to the airport and fly out in my little eagle."

"Did you refuel?" Ben wondered knowing the range of fuel would have been expended on the way down.

"Yea." Ezra said." I refueled but didn't pay yet. I was in the middle of the maintenance check when I saw the lady here and her armed guards so I stepped in."

Ben smiled. "I owe you one more."

"Yea." Ezra commented." I think I may have a way you can pay me back."

"What?" Ben questioned.

The Voice

"I'll let you know later." Ezra quipped.

Ezra had asked to see the Ark wanting to know first hand what he was getting into. He was raised orthodox, but no one had ever made a deal about the Ark from Solomon's Temple. As they approached the hiding place he sensed something different, it was almost as if there was an electrical current running through the ground. He didn't quite know what to make of it.

There was a sense of power, fierce and unforgiving. He felt like Moses walking on the Sinai when God had spoken. "Remove your shoes for you are standing on holy ground." All he could think of was how unworthy he was. Without any reminder, his life began to pass before him as if some one had made a trail of the sins he had committed. Every lie, stolen item, swear word, lustful thought came back and burned in his heart as if they were knives cutting to the quick. He stopped and motioned to Ben.

"What's wrong." Ben questioned, seeing Ezra bent over, his face a beet red and forehead pouring with perspiration. " Are you sick?"

It took Ezra a moment to even be able to speak. "I've got to get out of here. I'm too close to it. I'm looking at a film of my life and it's horrible."

Julie walked over to him and put her hands on his shoulder. "You need to realize that before God we are all guilty. You are just getting a glimpse of what it's going to be like on judgement day. Ezra, how are you going to be able to answer for your evil deeds?"

"I used to think my good deeds would outweigh my evil deeds, but I can't think of a single solitary thing I've done that was good." Ezra answered. "It's like I'm all evil and God knows it. He's got a record of my entire life. Even my thoughts. It's horrible."

"It's only horrible for those who haven't been forgiven and who stand naked before him, haunted by their very conscience. I have asked and accepted God's conditions for complete, entire forgiveness. I accepted the Lamb of God, the Messiah's death as payment for all my sins. When I stand before Him, He won't look

The Voice

at the evil I've done, He'll look instead at the sacrifice His Son made on my behalf. Ezra, you're trying to do it on your own and it's just not going to work. Don't be afraid of judgment, prepare for it and you'll find out it's a day for rejoicing, not of terror."

Ben walked over and put his hand on Ezra's shoulder. "I never thought I'd come to believe in Jesus, especially after the way I was raised, but He was as Jewish as you and me, and He was the Son of God and died for my sins and rose from the dead to prove it. I saw millions of tourists always going up to the empty tomb and I just ignored it, but when I finally asked myself why would so many people follow a hoax, I had to come face to face with my doubts and prejudices. It's not a hoax. Jesus rose from the dead. His first followers were all Jewish and for years they worshipped in the Temple until those who stood against God, wrapped up in their own self-righteousness and pride, created trouble for them and forced them underground. Ezra, I wouldn't be your friend if I didn't tell you to believe, to pray and accept the Messiah's forgiveness. Watch and you'll see your evil deeds disappear as if they had never happened. A weight will be lifted off of you."

"I'm ready." Ezra spoke. "I can't live with this guilt. I believe everything you're saying."

"Then pray with us, Ezra, and make the Messiah the ruler of your heart and this presence you feel will not make you nervous, but will fill you with joy even as it fills Ben and me." Julie added.

They all knelt on the path and prayed confessing their sins and listened as Ezra poured his heart out to God. Aeons away, God heard and that moment Ezra's transgressions were blotted out as if they had never happened. Ezra opened his eyes and the thoughts that had troubled his mind were gone. He was filled with an unbelievable peace and began to dance around to music playing only in his heart but with such rhythm that he couldn't still his feet. It was a moment of unbelievable joy and ecstasy. A glow emanated from his face and his tear ducts overflowed as he realized how real it was. He couldn't believe the simplicity of creating a relationship with his Creator, the God of the Universe, and part of him wondered why he didn't do so earlier, why he had waited so long to experience something so glorious.

CHAPTER EIGHT
Longing For Freedom

"They have tied me to a stake and I cannot fly." Shakespeare, Macbeth.

Ethiomu wandered down the deserted streets toward his new residence. Under his arms he could feel the ache of his lymph glands full of disease as his body rallied to fight off the dreadful bacteria that sought to turn his organs into breeding stations. He wondered how long it would be until he'd end up at the hospice. He was haunted by the look on his child's face as his wife had forced him out of the house. He had traded the love and respect of his children for fleeting moments of unbridled passion that had taken him faster to his deathbed than he ever would have imagined possible. His body was inebriated, but the thoughts of the death angel were so vivid that no amount of liquor could remove the terror that awaited him. He didn't even notice that in the background a Toyota driven by Wilbur was tailing him and barely reacted when it pulled up next to him.

"Ethiomu Habran?" The man spoke. "Get in. I need to have word with you."

Ethiomu got in the car and looked in the face of Wilbur Tonney.

"I know you." Ethiomu said.

"I imagine you do, Mr. Minister." Wilbur addressed him. "Look I'm going to get right to the point. I've been trailing you all night and I need your help. By the looks of it I think you need my help as well. A very important government official needs me to do a favor. You do me one I'll do you one."

The Voice

"What kind of favor?" Ethiomu responded, wondering what was in the bargain for him. 'What does a dying man need except another day?' He thought.

"I know you've got AIDS. You're walking death. You help me out, I'll get you into the U.S. for some experimental treatment. and the last years of your life will be as comfortable as possible. I can get you in the best program in our country, no charge to you. I know you're into the Saudi's for some big time favors but I need to know what moves they're having you make for them."

"They'll kill me if I say anything." Ethiomu responded. "But I'm a dead man anyway. Look, all I know is that they're after our one national treasure - The Ark of the Covenant. The King's nephew has died and now they're offering an unbelievable sum to keep the Ark from leaving the country."

"How much?" Wilbur said looking in his rear view mirror.

"Fifty million dollars." Ethiomu said. " They want me to verify whether or not it's the real thing. Only I've never seen the real thing. I told them I would be happy to. I don't know what you're doing down here but I got word they captured the American girl and she got away at the airport up in Aksum. No one knows how, but they suspect it was an Israeli pilot with his own courier jet. They're watching it. It will never leave Ethiopia. They've got stinger missiles standing by to shoot it out of the sky."

Wilbur grimaced. It was worse than he ever suspected. He was understaffed and under armed. He had a few friends with the National Freedom Party in Eritrea. They were combat men that had seen some pretty heavy action. He decided to pay them a visit in Massawa and see if they could help.

"You give this number a call when things get bad." Wilbur said. "Thanks for the information."

"In our country fifty million dollars represents unbelievable wealth and power. Even now the jackals are descending on Aksum." Ethiomu added with compassion. "I hope you are able to save your friend's children. God help them if they fall into the hands of the Saudis."

Wilbur went by private plane on an unscheduled flight to Massawa. It only took three hours and when he got off, the sun was beginning to come up on the Red Sea. The beauty and calmness of his surrounding belied to him the trap he was stepping into. When he was younger he had heard stories of the Ark. He knew one of King David's men had reached out to keep it from falling over when the cart it was in hit a gully by a stream and the man was instantly struck dead. He wondered what kind of God would choose to dwell in an Ark and what kind of fury the vessel would still possess. He thought with humor of the scene from "Raiders of the Lost Ark" and the Nazi's heads that exploded when they were exposed to the opened Ark. He knew that if someone had located the original artifact it would probably be one of the most monumental archaeological discoveries of all times reaffirming people's belief in the Bible. It was understandable to him why the Saudis, devout followers of Mohammed, would seek to destroy it.

The plane taxied down, sending Wilbur's head into the roof. He squeezed his large frame out of the cockpit and came face to face with Benebid Maki who towered over him. They both broke into big smiles.

"What is it now, Wilbur?" Benebid addressed him. "I hear nothing from you for three years and you call me in the middle of the night. It better be good. My wife is not a very happy woman, she enjoys my company much in the night hours."

"Well." Wilbur said slyly." I am sure you have made her happy on many, many nights. How well do you know Aksum?"

"As well as a man knows the path of his own cattle."

"There's some people up there I've got to try and get out. There is a trap planned for them at the airport and they probably know nothing of it."

Benebid pointed to his jeep, three men were in the back seat, their weapons in full sight. "Come, let us leave now. It will take us at least five hours, the roads are not good."

The Voice

The whole way to Aksum, they laughed and exchanged stories of the great war, the war which Benebid's people, outnumbered one hundred to one, had fought fiercely for independence from Ethiopia, battling from the rocks and crags of their mountainous country until the Ethiopians had grown weary. They had won because of additional help from people like Wilbur, who without official U.S. government sanction, had warned them time after time of government ambushes and guided them to caches of arms. Benebid would have paid him back with his life and Wilbur knew it. Their friendship bond ran deep and Wilbur knew if there was anyone who could help him rescue the Americans and Israelis it was Benebid's small yet deadly force.

Ben, totally unaware that help was on it's way, looked through Ezra's binoculars at the Aksum airport sitting calmly in the morning sun. Outside of a huge 707 with Arab markings, the airport seemed pretty dead. The wreckage of the other plane sat in a grassy field to the north of the runway. Ezra's plane sat off by itself not too far from a thick grove of trees and just off the main runway.

Rebu and Mori were down in the ravine with the Ark strung between two poles awaiting the word to march forward like warriors of old. Julie and Ezra were next to him trying to cover themselves from the bright rays of the sun threatening to expose their position.

"How does it look?" Julie said.

"It's too quiet." Ben responded. " What do you think?" Ben handed the glasses to Ezra.

Ezra studied the scene before him. He caught a reflection in the window of the cargo plane, the charred pavement was still visible where the remains of the torched jet had been parked. It was unusual that no one was around.

"It's ghost city." Ezra replied. "Unreal. Maybe they are waiting for us. Or maybe without the fuel truck to fill their planes they are just closed down. I say we go and try it. God is with us."

"God is with us, but it doesn't mean we give leave to our

common sense brother." Ben pointed out. "Let's not be too hasty. I'll have a word with Rebu and we'll see what's best."

Across the hill unseen to them, Wilbur was waiting with Benebid's men, one of Benebid's men had found out where the ambush had been laid for Ezra. It hadn't taken the Saudis long to find out through diplomatic channels that the jet belonged to an Israeli company. After that, they had laid a pretty sophisticated trap and they had even wired the plane with explosives.

Benebid looked through his binoculars and saw Julie, Rebu, Mori and Ben, and dispersed his men to meet them.

"What's up?" Wilbur asked, seeing the men leave.

"Look over to the left." Benebid said, directing his attention.

"I'll be a son of a pup." Wilbur exclaimed.

"Looks like they're going to try and get to the airport. That jet down there probably belongs to them."

"You gonna stop them."

Benebid nodded.

"Let's go." Ben spoke." The sun's glaring and it's going to be the only thing in our favor. Julie you stay here with Mori and the Ark. When you see we have control of the plane meet us down there as far away from the main building as possible. We'll load it up and take off."

"What if..." Julie began to say.

"Don't even say it. "Ben replied. "We don't have a backup plan."

"We're old hands at this Julie." Ezra smiled. "As long as the odds aren't more than fifty to one."

Benebid watched in horror as Rebu, Ben and Ezra worked the ridge line down towards the wire, he saw that his men would not reach them in time and knew he had to redeploy.

"Can you fly?" he asked Wilbur.

"Yea." Wilbur answered shocked.

"How about that?" Benebid pointed to the rather beat looking Arab 707 cargo plane covered with rust.

The Voice

"I can fly the question is. Does it fly?" Wilbur said.

"We're going to find out."

Benebid knew they had the element of surprise on their side. He knew the Saudi's wouldn't be ready for a two pronged attack and hoped to distract them long enough to allow the quarry to escape.

In the control tower Gerham Jabora was lazily watching the runway. It was the end of his shift and his eyes were tired and ached just to close. The morning sun rays felt like acupuncture needles and all he wanted was to close his eyes and escape to dream world. As he looked down he was horrified that right there beneath him the huge cargo plane was moving. The wing of the plane was heading for the building beneath him and crashed through the window, shattering glass waking up the sleeping interception forces. Unable to keep their vigil they had been awakened only to find debris all around them. They scurried about looking for their weapons but when they saw the huge plane bearing down on them they began to trample over one another looking for the door.

Ben and Ezra wondered who had come to their aid but gave it no second mind sprinting to the small jet. Ben pulled the landing blocks while Ezra started the engines and pulled down the runaway. Gerham watched in shock as the quarry made a run for it. He picked up his radio but found that the wires were dead. The cargo plane just slightly damaged was headed down the runway giving the jet cover.

Julie and Mori took the Ark between them and began to work their way down toward the fence where Rebu had cut a big hole. They were shocked to find soldiers in front of them.

Julie began to retreat but one of the tallest soldiers broke into a big grin and grasped one the poles and helped her with the Ark. The air around them was pulsating with visible electric current and out of nowhere a fog began to roll in. They were able to make out the shadow of the jet before them but all around the control tower visibility was reduced to less than three or four feet. Wilbur stopped the cargo plane fearing he'd run into the jet. They could hear the smaller jet's engines not too far away and went up to it just as the Ark arrived accompanied by the rest of their rescue team.

Before Julie could say anything, Wilbur extended his hand. "Your father sent me to help you. Look, I'm going to radio one of our carriers and see if I can't get you an escort back to Israeli airspace. But, just in case, tell them to fly low over the Red Sea, the Saudi AWACS will never pick you up on their radar."

Julie got on the plane with the Ark and waved a short goodbye. Before them, as miraculously as the Red Sea parting, the fog cleared and they sailed towards Israel.

Ben and Julie tied down the Ark securing it with bungee straps in the rear compartment.

"I've got to go to the bathroom." Ben exclaimed.

As he was sitting on the toilet he looked over and saw a bundle of plastic explosives and a timing device on them. He struggled pulling his pants back on and went out of the bathroom as if carried by a tornado.

"What's wrong?" Julie spoke. "You look white."

"The Saudi's have wired the plane with some kind of radio transmitter. I'm going to have to defuse the thing."

"Do you know how?" Julie asked with a look of puzzlement on her face.

"Just depends on how they have it wired. You only get one chance with these kinds of things. If it's radio operated we might not have much time. Get the electric repair kit from the cockpit. I'm going to give the thing another look."

On the ground the fog had lifted and the Saudi's had regrouped. They were still having trouble with their communication system. The transmitter that was to detonate the plane was lying in a heap of rubble. Four soldiers were gathered around it trying unsuccessfully to put it together. Medullah Sirronni, aide to the King, strolled in, surveyed the hopelessness and immediately boarded the royal helicopter which had been pulled out of the hangar. They had less than three hours to bring down the plane or he knew it would be his head on the block.

Wilbur and Benebid, after seeing the jet safely off, returned to Massawa. On the way Wilbur stopped at a pay phone and got himself connected to an overseas line. He used his password and before a minute had passed he was talking to Yokum Smarda, security chief of the Mediterranean section of the CIA. He explained what he needed and hung up the phone wondering whether or not Saudi influence would negate his request.

He walked back to the jeep.

"Well." Benebid spoke. "Are they giving your people air support?"

"I don't know." Wilbur. "The decision has got to be made much further up the ladder. The U.S. considers the Saudi's our best allies. We get half our oil from their country, and they spend their money buying lots of military hardware. They're pretty well entrenched. But anything can happen."

Israel was not without friends in the Defense Department. They knew the jet was in the air less than fifteen minutes later. Yokum Smarda made one phone call to a girlfriend in Reston, Virginia and within another ten minutes the word had filtered back to Israel that two of their citizens were fleeing with the Ark of the Covenant back to Israel. Airforce Chief of staff Judah BenZude, thought the situation through completely, he knew the small private plane was a sitting duck if the Saudi's got a reading on their radar scope He phoned Gideon Terpil on the Sinai. Gideon was the commander of a secret Israel radar location on the furthest southern point of the Sinai. Gideon dozing lazily in the shade, answered after several rings jarred him from his repose.

"Commander Gideon! This is General BenZude. Try and wake yourself up. We have a low flying jet returning back from Ethiopia. We need you to pinpoint its direction so we can provide some air support. This mission is vital to the safety and future survival of our country."

"Do you have the co-ordinates of the take-off site? " Gideon questioned pen in hand.

After Gideon got the co-ordinates he accessed the large transmitter which the Israelis had continually sweeping the southern Sinai. It registered every ocean and sea going vessel coming up through the Red Sea and the Suez and could detect and identify every plane large or small with the utmost accuracy. The Egyptians had the technology to do the same thing, but lacked the ability to run the complex computer programs that were necessary to make it work. Gideon had emigrated to Israel after finishing his computer science degree at Cal Poly. To the dismay of his parents and friends he had come back from a trip to Israel enthralled and feeling that he had found his place in life. The government had wasted no time in sending him into compulsory military service and they had found his extreme ability on the computers a real asset to their budding satellite operation.

Within fifteen minutes Gideon had the small plane on his tracking devices and was able to pull up a visual and transmit to Israeli Air Force headquarters the exact location of the plane. He could see the AWACS in the air that had flown out of Jeddah and knew that within twenty minutes the small jet would be in range of the AWACS and then it would be only a matter of time before one of the excellent Saudi pilots trained by the best instructors America had ever assembled would be on their tail and shooting them out of the sky.

General BenZude made a quick decision to send a squadron of Mirage Jets to meet and greet and escort them safely back. They were briefed and on their way within ten minutes. With the small plane so far away even at supersonic speeds time was still of the essence.

The squadrons in the Sinai and in Saudi Arabia took off at almost the same time, each headed for the same target. The Saudi's commands were clear - find and destroy. The Israeli's were also explicit - bring the Ark safely back so the Temple of Solomon could be rebuilt.

The Voice

While the small crew sat wondering and praying, Ben disengaged the bomb. Weary from all the excitement, Julie dozed off while gazing out the window at the wind driven whitecaps below her. At times she could almost feel the spray of the Red Sea misting up and cooling her face. She glanced over at the Ark wondering how a people with such history could have ever forsaken a God who actually opened up an entire sea to allow them out of slavery. As she drifted off to sleep travelling at over four hundred miles per hour, she was taken in a vision to the past splendors of Israel.

Solomon was dressed in robes befitting the richest king to have ever walked the earth. Gold threads were woven so finely they felt like silk. A sash of Royal purple decorated his trim waist. His beard slightly peppery in color trimmed in proper fashion rested upon his red tunic made of imported linen from Persia. There was no mistaking that he was the king. He glanced about him and his heart was proud. Proud of the wealth he had amassed in such abundant quantities that silver had become worthless. He accompanied the high priest towards the bronze altar. Blood had been flowing all day as before the altar animal after animal had been sacrificed to the Most High in atonement for the people's sins. Solomon stole a glance off to those packed in the Temple. Julie felt his eyes bearing into her heart and she thought he looked a bit like Ben. She turned aside to avoid being obvious. It was the only day that the high priest could actually go behind the curtain where the Ark rested. It was a gold chest placed on the altar. In it was the presence of the Most High. Solomon had never touched the Ark. No one had. It had been carried in a ceremony befitting the Most High God - on long poles made of acacia wood. They extended out far from the Ark itself allowing the priests to carry it without getting too close. Solomon recalled the story of his father David transporting it on a cart and Uzzah reaching out to support the Ark as the oxen stumbled going through a river bed. He died instantly. David had gotten mad at God and named the place "attack on Uzzah."

The Voice

Solomon knew the city of his father was blessed because of the presence of the Ark. It was clear to him that God's presence had brought peace and prosperity to everyone. He turned to address the crowd.

"Today we dedicate this Temple, a Temple where the presence of the Most High shall dwell." He lifted his arms towards Heaven and declared. "Oh Lord God of Israel who is like unto thee? You have been faithful to Your servant David by allowing his son to build You this house where You may dwell, and You have kept all Your promises to him. There is no room in all of Heaven, O Lord how can You possibly live in this temple. Yet, You have chosen to dwell with us, Your people, even as you promised Moses. Oh Lord don't take Your presence from us. We are a stubborn and rebellious people forgive us our transgression and don't blot our names out of Your most holy book"

When Solomon had finished praying a Holy Fire came down from the sky and the sacrifices which lay before the altar were instantly consumed. A dazzling glory filled the Temple and all the people worshiped the Lord. That day alone over twenty two thousand cattle and a hundred thousand sheep were sacrificed. As the priests blew on their trumpets and the Levites played their musical instruments the people worshiped and stayed for fourteen days, no one leaving to go home. On the twenty third day of that month, the seventh month of the year, Solomon sent them home. No one was sad.

Julie awoke as Ezra banked the plane sharply to the left. A Saudi patrol boat had popped up suddenly on the horizon and he had almost crashed into the tower. Within minutes the captain was reporting the low flying plane to headquarters. The Saudi's had a lock on him and were less than two minutes away from intercept. Ben looked back at Julie who had been startled from her dream.

"Jules." Ben said. "We've been spotted. If you ever prayed now's the time to do it. "

"You mean now's the time we do it." Julie replied. Ezra leaned forward, seeing if he could get anymore speed out of the aircraft. The gravitational pull at the low altitude was taking its toll on the engines which were running hotter than he would have liked.

"Ben. " Ezra stated, watching the condensation roll down the front windshield. "It looks like we have a storm front coming."

"That's impossible." Ben replied. "I've been watching, there's not a cloud around for miles."

Overhead the waiting Saudi squadron flew. The private jet was no match for them in speed or in any other capacity. The squadron leader had watched as the tiny radar blip had disappeared in a cloud. Without notice a large jet stream suddenly appeared as if out of nowhere extending up nearly a mile in height and was travelling at hurricane speeds. The F-15's directly overhead found themselves being tossed to and fro, as if they were feathers caught in an updraft. They were flying in a tight wing formation - the leader in the middle and the other planes wing to wing. The squadron commander looked in horror as his wing hit into the plane next to him sending it into a tailspin but not before the pilot who had over-corrected had been broad sided by the next plane. Before the commander had known it half of his plane was in flames and he was struggling to navigate in a severe electrical storm, Unknowingly, and without warning he had led his squadron into total darkness. He tried to relay to the others to break off but the static on his radio prevented him from communicating to the point they could understand him. It took him a minute to realize that his automatic pilot computer was shorted out and he didn't have the slightest idea what direction he was travelling.

He broke through the cloud just moments before descending into the Red Sea. His two remaining pilots followed him close behind. The planes crashed with amazing force, breaking apart upon impact and sending huge geysers of steam and water into the sky.

Ezra had no idea what was happening all around him. He had heard about the cloud that had followed the Israelites when they left

Egypt and which the Lord had used to lead them forty years through the wilderness, when they refused to enter the promised land. He had heard, but he had never expected to be in it. Every evil thought and deed he had ever done rose in his mind as if his memory bank had transferred all data to the present. He felt the presence of the Almighty God, Supreme Being, a presence so holy it was as if fire was consuming his very bowels.

Julie was full of awe. She could sense the presence but instead of being repelled by her own sense of unworthiness she was drawn to it and allowed the presence to fill her to a point of overflowing. Each cell in her heart and mind overflowed with electrical currents of love. At peace with herself and at peace with her Creator, she looked at the Ark next to her and saw a stream of light burrow itself back into the box as if the gold lid covering it had allowed the light waves through. It was like suspended molecular movement. She sensed for the first time the awesomeness of the Creation - how out of nothing, God had made all. She felt drawn to the Compassionate One who had not only created mankind in His image and likeness but also died and made a way for man to have fellowship with Him without guilt. It was beyond words and she could do no more than bask in the afterglow of her Creator's presence.

Ben looked back at her, curious about the light emanating from her face. He found his mouth unable to open.

Overhead, a squadron of Israeli Mirage jets were searching for them.

"Bravo, bravo." The lead pilot spoke. "We have visual contact repeat. Advise."

"Good news Telios." The dispatcher spoke. "Predator's gone for a swim. Bring the little bird back to nest..."

Telios slowed down and flew next to Ezra making sure that Ezra could see the star of David. He made a motion to follow and Ezra acknowledged. Within ten minutes they were on the ground and the ground crew was rolling out camouflage nets and covering up the aircraft.

The base commander walked out to greet them. Gideon, a man of large physical proportion with a robust nose and bushy black hair extended his hand and smiled warmly.

"Welcome home." he greeted and was shocked to see Julie with them. Ben was amused at his reaction."

"Commander." Ben spoke. " Please allow me to introduce you to Julie Reinhold and Ezra..."

"Yes." Gideon smiled even broader." You don't have to introduce me to this rascal. Who else could fly in broad daylight through enemy lines at six hundred miles an hour just a few feet over the water. Good to see you Ezra. The General insists you wait for a larger escort. Please come into my quarters, we'll have something cool and you can tell me all about your discovery."

CHAPTER NINE
The World Awaits

General BenZude flew to the Sinai with the squadron to personally oversee the transportation of the Ark to Jerusalem. He stepped off the plane into the hot sun and squinted up wondering why there were no clouds. He looked at the desolation about him and tried to think what it must have been like for his forefathers travelling by foot from Egypt. He laughed when he realized that they could reach Egypt in fifteen minutes and his forefathers had wandered about forty years until the entire older generation had died and Jehovah had started with a fresh group. As he approached Gideon's headquarters he caught a glimpse of the American girl. His heart skipped a beat. She reminded him of his wife when he'd met her on the coast of the Mediterranean thirty five years earlier. He could hear laughing and celebration outside of the room.

The commander stood at attention the moment the General stepped into the room. The civilians looked up at him with a puzzled reaction and began to get to their feet as well.

"At ease everyone." The General spoke. "This is like a day of rejoicing." He glanced at Julie's face wondering how it got such a glow.

"Thank you General." Julie spoke extending her hand. "For safely orchestrating our return to Israel. We know you met with some opposition."

"I understand from the commander you disappeared in a cloud that came out of nowhere, not unlike my ancestors."

Ben stood to his feet. "General BenZude, this is Julie Reinhold. A woman of extraordinary courage."

"Like old Golda, hey?" The general reminisced. "Yes." He shook both their hands. "Well, maybe you'll think of settling here close to your beloved Ark."

"I've got direct orders from the Prime Minister that you are both to be given a special reception tonight and our highest decoration." He turned his attention to Ezra. "You as well, Ezra. Now where is this Ark?"

"We thought it best not to disturb it." Ben replied looking to Julie for reassurance. "It's still in the jet. We don't have the necessary poles to use in moving it off the plane..."

"What he's trying to say General. It might be a religious artifact, but it's definitely something with an extraordinary presence. Can't you see my face, if you turn the light off you will see how I glow. There's power in it, Sir, and we're unsure of just how to treat it, so we opted for the way they used to treat it, and in those day no one was allowed to touch it. They carried it about on poles made of acacia wood. For some reason God has decided to unveil this Ark and He definitely doesn't want anyone messing with Him. All due respect," she added.

"Very sound advice." the General replied. "I'll make sure then when we arrive at Jerusalem airport that there are bearers with Acacia wood poles to carry the Ark."

The word had leaked out to the Jerusalem Post of a secret mission and of several Saudi planes that had crashed not too far from the Sinai in hot pursuit. The press and photographers were packed five deep around the perimeters of the Jerusalem airport. Security was tight but people had climbed the fence hoping for a better look The reputation of Ben Gibron was well known, the Israeli treated their archaeologists like celebrities anyway and with his dashing figure and handsome features, he had more than his share of popularity.

The government had decided to have the Ark carried from the plane by the rabbinical students of the Orthodox church. When the plane landed, the red carpet was rolled out and Ben and Julie stepped out to the cheers of the crowd. They stepped aside as an honor guard standing at arms walked up and lined up on both sides of the carpet. Four rabbinical students came out and managed to get their poles into the plane and slowly manipulated the Ark out of the aircraft. The sun was overhead at twelve o'clock and the Ark glowed as it was bathed in the warm yellow rays. Hundreds of cameras went off and videos from news reporters all over the world were recording the momentous event. A hum started from the Ark that was audible to all. All around people could feel the power coming from the ancient relic. As they took the Ark through the honor guard, they passed an elderly lady severely disfigured. The reflective rays of the Ark bathed her in a golden glow and she got up out of her wheelchair healed.

"I'm healed." She cried jumping to her feet in front of everyone. The crowd was stunned and crushed in on her to touch her. Israeli soldiers formed a guard around her and escorted her away from the Ark as she continued to proclaim her miracle.

Ben turned and faced Julie. "This is the most important thing that has ever happened since the establishing of the nation Israel. Look at these people, a new devotion to the true God has filled their hearts, just like in the times of old. Surely they will welcome the Messiah this time when He returns."

"Yes." Julie replied. "I believe they will. In spite of the thousands of troops poised on the borders of your small country just waiting to annihilate you, your people still have faith."

"They know God brought us back here and not to be destroyed, but to worship Him in spirit and in truth. He hasn't finished with His chosen people. Even though we are but a remnant we are still His chosen. Nothing could ever take that away from us."

"Yes, Ben." She smiled, holding his arm as they were driving away from the crowd. "He has chosen you and you have chosen Him. God has a wonderful plan for you. What will they do with the Ark?"

"They have already made arrangement to put it in the Art Museum. It has a state-of-the-art security system and they will allow some people to see it and then it will be installed back in the rebuilt temple."

She looked out the window at the narrow roads and marvelled at how she was driving on the very streets where Jesus had walked. She couldn't keep her mind from wandering and drifted back to the time when Jesus had been hailed by thousands of people only a week before He was scourged and crucified. She wondered if everyone was that excited about seeing the Ark returned.

* Rome *

Not everyone was interested in seeing the Jewish Temple rebuilt. His official title was Defender of the Faith but he was really a glorified hit man. Ignacio Robella didn't even have to consult with those above him at the Vatican. He knew they would view the return of the Ark the same way he viewed it - as a threat to the Vatican's intentions which hadn't changed since the crusades - to establish Jerusalem as a Holy City for Roman Catholicism and its eight hundred million followers. He intended to make sure that the Temple would never be rebuilt. He had unlimited funds to do so and a list of agents worldwide he could call on at any time to help further his agenda.

After he had heard the news on CNN, he immediately booked

The Voice

a flight from Rome to Jerusalem. He contacted his agent and made sure to have all the munitions available to him the moment he landed. He had been in and out of over twenty countries supervising assassinations, bombings of Mosques and churches. He never traveled using his real passport and he was quite confidant that his identity was still a highly guarded secret known only to the one man he answered to. He slammed the door of the taxi and walked to the front entrance of the airport. In front of him was a young priest who had stopped to bless a small infant held in the arms of a modestly dressed village woman. He stopped to look at the scene and passed by. For a moment he had seen himself in all his innocence but the picture was too distant to have any real meaning to him.

He had over an hour before his departure and stopped to get a cappuccino and sweet bread. The television was on and a woman was being interviewed talking excitedly about being healed from cancer while in the presence of the Ark. Ignacio dismissed it as random hysteria. He didn't believe in healing or miracles. He only believed in what he could see. He regretted the loss of his childlike faith that had caused him long ago to take his vows and wondered if his departed mother, the most godly woman who ever lived, knew that joining the priesthood would have made him an assassin and a man who had already lost his own soul while trying so desperately to insure the salvation of so many others.

He glanced down at his watch and got up leaving a generous tip. He glided down to the security gate where his weapon disguised as a shaving kit and hair dryer made it through without a hitch. He smiled at the wonders of common technology. If he had a god anymore, it was technology. The ability to destroy was perhaps mankind's most supreme achievement. He had held small plastic explosives that could bring down entire superstructures. He knew the power to destroy far outweighed the power to build. He chided himself for being too philosophical and boarded the plane.

He had a window seat and looked over the blue water of the

Mediterranean Sea. He was surprised at how translucent it was and how tranquil it appeared. The sea was dotted with luxury liners, steamers and small sailing and fishing vessels. He thought of how small they all appeared. They had no idea of why he was going to Jerusalem but would all hear about it soon enough. The thought gave him some satisfaction.

CHAPTER TEN
Your Soul Is Required

Ethiomu woke up in a pool of blood. He had never made it back to America for the excellent care as promised by the CIA. Instead he had sought comfort at one their own AIDS centers, the one he had visited when he first learned he had the disease. He could feel the stickiness all over his chest and matted in his hair. Throughout the night his body, ravaged by disease, had surrendered to the virus. Everywhere his body had mounted a defense against it, his t-cell count, drastically low, had failed to rid his body of the danger. He was hopelessly outnumbered and defenseless against the viruses which were multiplying at an astonishing rate. His gums had been attacked the worst and had poured forth an oozing combination of pus and blood. He hadn't the strength to even lift his head out of it. He attempted to move but found his arm pinned under him. He heard muffled footsteps and the light went on. A hand moved his head gently and brushed his forehead. It was the hand of God. He had never known God in a real personal way and was touched by the compassion shown to him. Somehow he could hear the still small voice speaking to his heart telling him he was loved. At one time he had found God unapproachable. He marveled after looking his whole life, he had finally come to know the love that God offered while he was stretched out on a cot in an AIDS Hospice.

A gentle hand passed a cool washcloth over his head cleaning out the matted blood contaminated with enough of the virus to infect the entire city of New York.

"There." Bridgette spoke. "We need to keep a better look out on you. Ethiomu, you know that things aren't looking up for you. Your body has little or no defense left against this virus and there's no drug that can help you."

She looked into his eyes and he nodded.

"Why don't you take this time to cleanse your heart before God. You know Christ paid for all your sins. There's no need to stand before his judgment seat guilty. If you pray with me He can forgive them now and when you die, He'll welcome you into heaven. Wouldn't you like that?"

Bridgette stifled back a cough. She had feared someday she would catch the virus but her love for God and the calling on her life made it seem like nothing compared to being there for people who had no hope left. She had refused a test but knew that a test would show her carrying the virus. She had seen the death a thousand times and each time it had taken on a different face but the results were always the same; pain, discomfort, unconsciousness and finally rest. She looked down affectionately at the frail man lying in front of her and remembered the first time he had come in, afraid to reveal the real reason, but she had known. She had known that one day he would be lying in her hospice and had prayed many times that he would overcome the pride in his heart and embrace the forgiveness God offered. She felt a small squeeze. Ethiomu had finally given in. The battle inside of him at last had been decided.

"You want to pray for forgiveness. " She asked looking in his eyes clouded in pain.

He winked and a tear floated from the side of his eye.

"Just agree with me Ethiomu. God doesn't need to hear your voice. He can hear your heart. He can see you turning away from those things which destroyed you."

As she prayed, a soft presence came over him again as if his very being was cleansed, like water from a mountain stream would course its way through the rocks loosing all the contaminated particles. His guilt and shame began to drop away and he felt a real hope well up in his heart, a hope that his life wouldn't be for nothing, that somehow by his death he could help change the lives of others. He prayed to God for strength to use his life for one more day.

Miraculously the virus subsided, by the end of the week Ethiomu was back in health walking through the ward cheering up others. A true testimony to the power of God. He approached Bridgette.

"Miss Bridgette. " he said looking at her. "You didn't have to do this type of work. Why have you risked your life to help us? We're not even your people. We're Africans. You could be in Germany enjoying the good life."

"Apart from God there is no life for me. When I was a little girl I answered God's call to me to be a nurse and help others. This is where he brought me."

"But when you're gone?"

"Then I pray that He'll bring someone else to carry on. This epidemic is not going to end. Maybe another little girl right now is praying to God for direction in her life just like I prayed. I'm not saying I was happy then with what he told me to do. I wanted a husband, children, a normal life but if you ask me now, would I go live my life a different way, be rid of this virus? No. My reward is those like you who the Lord has allowed me to direct back to His flock."

"I have decided to write my memoirs. I called my secretary and she will be coming down writing things down until I'm finished. I was wondering..."

"Yes." Bridgette smiled. " I've already heard from the Lord. We'll print them up and give them to young people in the schools and universities. I'm sure it will be wonderful."

Ethiomu busied himself in between visits by his secretary with putting down his memoirs, he also poured over scripture passages to include in his book. Bridgette served as his editor helping him select stories and getting him to divulge as much of himself as he could. She had no doubt the book would cause a big sensation. Coptics had long regarded themselves as followers of Christ but most had abandoned true religion of the heart and had just carried out hollow rituals that were meaningless to God.

After a week Ethiomu felt his final strength again ebbing away. Bridgette sat next to him rubbing his forehead with a damp cloth trying to bring him comfort.

"It's a miracle I lived this much longer isn't it?"

"Yes." She replied."You've beat all the odds."

Ethiomu pressed a note into her hands. "I'd like you to give it to my wife and daughters. The address is inside. I need to die with a clear conscience."

"I understand." Bridgette said. "I've already talked to your wife and children and told them how sick you are. They're coming by today. "

Ethiomu waited the rest of the day wondering what they were going to think of him. He had read most of the Bible and had seen the passage that stated. "Your sins shall find you out." He had seen first hand that his had. His years of cheating on his wife with many females had taken its toll. He thought about all the good he could have done for his country with his wealth and power and how instead he had squandered it on his lusts. They all seemed so meaningless to him as he watched his life ebbing away. He drifted off to sleep and began to dream.

He was in a field. All around him people were sweating, roasting in the sun's rays, being scorched. He was walking up and down the field spooning out water from his bucket. Everyone got more than enough to drink and yet his bucket seemed to remain full. He understood that there was no limit to love and that what he was accomplishing in his last few days on earth would have true significance. It was a warming thought.

He drifted off to a deeper sleep. He looked down and saw his wife and daughters gathered around his bed. His wife was reading the note he had left her. He could see her crying and the children comforting her. He felt a light touch on his shoulder. he turned to see a beautiful face.

"Come, Ethiomu." The being spoke. "We have a place for you. It's time."

"But my wife?" He challenged. "Will she be okay? My daughters they have no father."

"God will be their father. Your good deeds will live on. Come."

Ethiomu saw the world decrease until it was a tiny speck. The air seemed to open in front of him and he heard trumpets so loud that he was taken aback and expected his ears to hurt. He looked down at his wasted body and saw it was whole again. There was a joy that filled his being in such a tremendous way that all the memories of the pain, heartbreak and disappointment were gone. The sound of the trumpets grew louder, mixed with the sound of a powerful wind. As he got closer he realized that it wasn't wind at all but untold numbers of voices joined together. He found himself floating towards the center of the throng. He could still distinguish the different races and was surprised so many were present. The words that everyone were singing seemed familiar to him and without second thought he joined in the chorus paying homage to the Creator of the universe. He knew things couldn't get any better.

"Mrs. Hagid." Brigette tried to rally her out of her remorse."He's not coming back to this earth, but I promise you. You can see him again."

"If only I wouldn't have made him leave." She spoke sobbing holding on to her two daughters as if a fierce wind would rip them away also.

"No. " Bridgette spoke in reassurance. "You did the right thing. It was God's plan that he come here and that we prepared him for his final journey. As you see from the note, he was prepared. Wasn't he?"

"Yes." She said cheering up a bit. "How can we ever see him again, He's gone he's not coming back."

Bridgette pointed beyond the ceiling where the fan was blowing cold air around.

"You can see him there. He had an appointment like all of us. You can prepare for your appointment and see him there if you're ready. Would you like to? You need to repent of your sins as well, claim God's forgiveness. Your hatred of your husband, even though he wronged you, was a sin. You need to ask God to forgive you for your hate."

"I don't hate him anymore." She responded and dropped to her knees to pray. "God, I'm so sorry for my anger. I'm sorry for holding back affection towards my husband for all those years for being demanding and driving him out of my bed. Forgive me God. Thank you for dying for my sins, for Christ's death on the cross. I need..."

Beyond the earth her prayers were heard and Ethiomu's heart filled with even more joy as the knowledge of his wife's salvation filtered up to him.

The story that Ethiomu had written was printed and distributed all over Ethiopia. his wife took over the distribution and personally answered the hundreds of letter that came from people seeking the peace and forgiveness of God. Each time another person made a decision to seek God, Ethiomu's happiness increased.

Moussaud's spirit was wandering over the Ethiopian countryside. There was no rest for it. He was aware he no longer had a physical body but didn't know how to process the information. He knew there were others looking for him. Twice he had barely managed to escape from those whom he knew would bring him to an even more dreadful death.

His luck was not to last much longer. Rothar, the spirit that had exercised influence over him, driving him to incredible vile acts of torture and murder was intent on finding him and tormenting him. The spirits loathed their loss of the Ark and the attention it was bringing the Creator.

Rothar looked out over the Ethiopian wasteland. It was night and he sensed the presence of a his former host close by. It was as if he could smell the rotting carcass of a heart so black with sin that the stench it gave off was unbearable. It was a smell that he had grown attracted too. He stretched his long webbed fingers and leaned back and howled as if he were a ravenous wolf. His hair was long and unkempt and hung in long dreadlocks to the middle of his back, hardened with the fires of hell that had tempered it and given his skin a lacquered look - black and shiny. His eyes, inhuman, had a distinct reptilian nature to them almost a reddish orange hue and out of them came no light, no mercy, no love.

He was a being of incalculable cruelty. A nightmare beyond human contemplation. Dead, yet alive, his only goal was to torture and maim his former host, punishing him for his untimely death.

Moussaud had found a large tree, full of leaves where the country women had frequently come to collect leaves and sticks for their small cooking fires. He had made up a dwelling place in the middle of the trunk and wanted nothing more than to be left alone. He was tormented by the thoughts of the evils he had committed during his short and misdirected life. He could sense around him the presence of a great evil and chose to remain frozen in the tree.

Any other demon would have given up and passed him by but the spirit that was hunting him was relentless as a cold Siberian wind. Rothar sniffed about and smelled the fear which emanated from Moussaud's diseased spirit. The claws reached into the tree and found him. He cried in pain as the rough hands drug him out into the moonlight.

"You can't hide forever." Rothar spoke revealing a mouthful of rot.

"Why don't you just leave me be." Moussaud pleaded. "I did your bidding here on earth I'm sure there are other things I can do for you now that I am invisible."

"Yes." Rothar laughed. "You can serve as entertainment for us while we torture you and hear you beg for mercy."

The trip down to the sulfuric fiery sea happened so fast that Moussaud was there almost instantly. The first thing that assaulted his senses were the voices. They seemed to cry out from everywhere. Moans and distress unlike anything he had ever witnessed filled his ears and filled him with terror. The claws, which had gripped him tightly, loosed him and he was guided to a group of creatures sitting around a woman who was bound and being poked with long spears of molten metal. Her mouth had been propped open and a funnel had been forced down her throat. One of the creatures had taken a bucket of hot molten lava and had begun to empty it into her mouth. Moussaud looked on in horror.

"Pleasant isn't it. She thought for years she was getting away with all her lying and deceit but here we get to mete out punishment." Rothar spoke

"She was a liar?"

"Yes but there was one person she could never lie to. He gave her chance after chance to change and she didn't, but only got worse. A car wreck claimed her mortal life and we took her immortal soul."

Rothar marched him down to a large open arena. It looked like a grotesque gladiator circus. Beings were dressed in all types of metal breastplates, helmets and wielded axes, spiked balls and chains, scimitars, lances. In the middle of the arena was a group of men and women huddled together. Surrounding the arena were many watching, who had died at the hands of those being tortured. They were screaming for vengeance."

"Those who live by the sword will die by the sword." Rothar opened a gate and thrust him in.

"Wait." Moussaud cried. "You don't expect me to face them with no weapon - defenseless."

"That's how your victims were, weren't they? Why should it be any different for you? It's your turn. Let the games begin." Rothar shouted.

The Voice

The carnage was swift and violent. Those who in their past lives were the tormentors were the tormented. Legs and arms were hacked off and bodies drug around while those in the stands threw rocks at them. Several had their heads severed from their bodies and were batted about gaping in horror as they realized that even though they were decapitated they were every bit alive. Moussaud was impaled on a spear running up through his rear. Bit by bit a reptilian creature began to chew off his feet. He cried out to Allah to save him and a large imposing creature came to him.

"I am Allah." the thing spoke. "You have your reward now. This is your paradise. You and the millions of others who sought to serve me by the shedding of blood and vengeance."

"But you were supposed to take us to an eternal abode of blessing. I died in battle for your cause."

The creature laughed in a voice that rumbled the ground. Its head was as large as a cobra and its tongue darted back and forth."

"I lied." It laughed. "This is my abode and now I share it with you. It bothers me to hear you scream my name."

A claw reached in his mouth and extracted his tongue. It was a bloody stump with roots and all and was held in front of him. Moussaud could no longer even scream he just moaned.

"You are one of the damned. You followed a lie and now you must live with its consequences."

The huge claw picked him up stake and all and held him far over its head. "Behold one of your tormentors. You wanted vengeance."

The limp body of Moussaud was thrown into the stands where it stuck in the ground upside down. Moussaud felt the rushing of hands and teeth as every area of his being was bitten and clawed and his very spirit ripped in shreds. He had never known such pain was even possible and he remembered those he had tortured wondering if they had felt as he did.

As Rothar turned around he ran into Allah.

"You failed your mission. You were to stop the Ark from being discovered. Now many are turned away from Islam and embracing the Christian god.

"I will give you one more chance or you too will end up as him. There is one who can still stop the Ark from being authenticated. Go and aid him and perhaps you will live to see another day"

"Yes Allah." Rothar bowed in the traditional salute touching his chest, his lips, and his forehead.

CHAPTER ELEVEN
The Holy Sea

Ignacio's flight over the Mediterranean was for the most part uneventful. The threat of Palestinian terrorists taking over had died down since Khaddafi had decided to quit giving them asylum and instead had them executed. As Ignacio looked down he could see faint whitecaps and container ships. He marvelled at how many goods from China and the Far East were transported by sea through the Suez and up through the Mediterranean. He thought of his humble young days when he had worked in Ancio sponge fishing with his father and uncles until modern sponge factories had put them out of business and into the poor house. He wondered what life would have been like if he had married his teenage sweetheart Alana instead of joining the priesthood to give his family one less mouth to feed. Father Ignacio they all called him now. They were proud of him, the whole village turned out every time he went to visit his aging mother and aunt. His mom bragged about her son at the Vatican. He wondered what she would think if she knew what really he did.

Special Emissary they called him. He preferred to think of it as "dirty deeds done dirt cheap." He wondered what God really thought of him making other people's lives miserable. He wasn't sure when he had grown evil towards other people because he could never remember a real time in his life where he had given and shared love, except the brief period with Alana and they had all stolen that from him. He glanced down at his onyx cross, a final gift from his father when he was ordained. "Blessed are the simple" he thought for their minds are protected from evil ways. He had read about the inquisition and had wished the days would return when those who disobeyed the Pope would not only be excommunicated, but tortured as well. In his opinion, the church had given too much leeway to too many and the time to wield an iron fist had returned. The discipline at seminary had hardened him beyond the breaking point. Whatever last vestiges of love that had been in him before, his first class had pounded, molded, and burnt it out of him. He fancied himself as a soldier of God and those who disobeyed Holy Mother Church were his sworn enemies. "Recant or die a heretic" was his motto. There was no room for forgiveness or tolerance.

Although he had never personally killed anyone he knew that orders he had given to others had caused men to die. It didn't bother him. Nothing got through the thick veneer. After thirty years in the priesthood, all but five years spent at the Vatican, nothing bothered him. He had survived though the Pontiffs had come and gone, he had worked his way up to the top and was answerable to no one. He knew that the Pontiff wished to be left ignorant of his activities. His job was to protect in whatever way he saw fit the interests of the church. If heads rolled no one wanted the blood rolling over their toes. He understood that although the church promised absolution, the ends justifying the means, in the end, he was alone answerable to God.

That's what bothered him. Call it a stream of conscience. Since the Vatican physician had told him to lay off the brandy and he had become more health conscious, his mind had cleared and he could no longer fog up his mind with alcohol trying to escape from the effects his deeds had made on his own memory bank. He had sought absolution visiting out of the way churches and going through confession, but he felt bound to his past like a Roman slave was bound to the galleys before their battles. He could feel the fires of hell. It was almost as if Satan was laughing at him, stoking the flames giving him a foretaste of the weight that guilt carried. The habits could not be broken. Anytime something threatened the church as the discovery of the Ark did by giving credence to the Jewish faith and giving them a cornerstone on which to rebuild their temple, his response was automatic. Neutralize. He had taken the words out of the vocabulary that identified his actions as sins and whitewashed them so they appeared differently. He had in essence...lied to himself, only his conscience was not buying the lies anymore. His heart was in rough shape. He was still a good forty pounds overweight and could not give up his chain smoking. With a head as bald as a cue ball and beaked nose, Ignacio most resembled a vulture. That's what they called him behind his back, 'Vultura'. It was an apt description.

After the news broke, Robert Sweeney got back in touch with Wilbur Tonney. John Reinhold was still too sickly for the long flight over to Jerusalem and John called on his old friend for another favor.

"Robert." Wilbur answered, "You really think it's necessary. I'm sure the Israelis got her covered pretty good. I've still got some loose ends to tie up here and I'm trying to keep an eye out for any new Saudi developments."

"I've got first rank clearance, Wilbur. The action has moved and everyone feels that since you know the players, you should quarterback this thing until it stabilizes. When can you get up there?"

"No official flack," Robert responded. "I'll have a pouch for you at the Embassy in Israel for your eyes only. We value our Israeli partners. They're crazy, but not as bad as the two hundred million fanatics around them. Look, when the girl returns, I want you to be her unofficial shadow. Word has it she's coming back soon with some very incredible artifacts. You make sure you arrive with her."

"Got you," Wilbur said. "Her old man must have pulled some pretty big strings."

"Let's just say the autoworkers still do a lot of voting and his years in labor relations made him some pretty loyal friends. He lost one child over there, he doesn't want to lose the other one."

Gale Wallace answered the phone looking out at the gnarled oak tree in the backyard in Dearborn.

"Hello," she answered.

A voice echoed back.

"Gale, Gale," Julie said.

"Julie," Gale responded. "We're so sorry to hear about Doug's death. Your father phoned me a bit ago and told me what happened. Your father is like a new man, all he can talk about is Jesus. He even came to the Wednesday night prayer meeting."

"I'm coming back at the end of the week," Julie gushed out. "There's so much to tell you. It's unbelievable."

"I saw you on television. It's all anyone is talking about. We've had floods of inquiries. Jack has had to add on several phone lines and get volunteers to handle the volume of phone calls. Is it really true you found the ten commandments?"

"Yes," Julie said. "They were right inside the Ark, Ben promised me I could take them back for analysis. Rumor has it because they've got their Ark back, they're going to finally get going on the Temple construction."

"They're not getting upset that you are going to analyze the tablets?"

"No one has said anything because Ben brought it in from another country where it was taken knowingly years ago and they know it belongs to him. If he doesn't want to, he doesn't even have to leave it in Israel. In fact, he's already talking to several exhibitors about touring the Ark, the interest is unbelievable," Julie gushed.

"I imagine it is especially after that healing," Gale said. "Julie, something has me worried. I was praying for you and I felt this dark cloud. I don't think you are aware of the danger you are in."

The Voice

Julie thought a moment and knew that often times when they prayed together Gale had visions.

"I know what you're saying...finding this Ark was only a small part of the battle. If this thing was hidden for so many years, then..."

Gale interrupted, "I'm not going to beat around the point, the Lord showed me that you are coming under attack, first from your brother and then your father."

"What happened to my father?" Julie said.

"He had a heart attack and died," Gale said. "It's a miracle that he's even alive. He claims that Jesus sent him back to finish his life's work. I don't imagine anyone said anything to you. We'll call a special time of prayer and fasting for your protection. Remember it's Satan that wants to destroy you and Ben. Beware of pride, it'll bring you down faster than anything else. Call me back soon. I've got to run now. I love you."

"I love you too." Julie hung up and walked to the elevator and back up to her room. As she looked out the lobby window a dark shadow passed. Overhead flight #343 Rome to Jerusalem circled waiting for landing clearance.

She knocked on Ben's door and was surprised to see it open. A large American man extended his hand.

"Miss Reinhold. I'm Wilbur Tonney. Special attaché with the American Embassy," he smiled.

"Nice to meet you," she said.

"I understand that you'll be returning to the United States to do a scientific analysis on the Ten Commandment tablets. I'm just going to make sure nothing happens to you or them and that you arrive on U.S. soil safely. I'll be sort of your guardian angel. You won't even know I'm around most of the time. I wanted to let you know so you wouldn't think someone was following you. I'd prefer it if you'd just act as you normally would and not draw any attention to me."

"Julie," Ben said, "I think it's a good idea. We'll need

109

somebody watching out for us when we go back to the states."

"We?" Julie was puzzled. "But your work is here."

"My work here is done," Ben said. "My scientific papers and account I can write anywhere. Besides what is science without testing? You can give the scoffers of the world a true chance to examine your data. Prove the age of the tablets and see if your theory can be proven. We already have a geologist bringing some samples from the Sinai Desert that we can take along with us for comparative analysis."

"Do you mind, Miss Reinhold," Wilbur said, "If I ask you what type of analysis you'll be doing?"

"Is that an official or non-official question?" Julie responded, bothered that Big Brother was going to be looking over her shoulder.

"Unofficial." He responded without even thinking.

"I plan on proving to the world that these Ten Commandments were actually given to us by God. Did you know that most people can't name but a few of them. Our society in general has forgotten about them. We remain grossly ignorant of them and as a consequence, we degrade further and further every year. While population increases in small increments, crime increases at unfathomable proportions. Soon we'll be a nation of prisons and detention facilities. We have more people in prison than Russia did during their worse purges. It may be great for the prison industries, but when twenty percent of black males are incarcerated, it makes the raising of children an extremely difficult task."

"You suppose your papers will make a difference?" Wilbur was serious, not just goading her.

"I'm a scientist, Mr. Tonney, my approach is one of science, but I'm also a Christian and if God gives me the grace to show the world the error of their ways in ignoring His wishes, then I am doing what He placed me here for."

Ignacio woke up from his short daydream when the jet tires skidded down on the airport runway. He was happy for his various diplomatic passports and his ability to go in and out of countries without having to walk through metal detectors or customs inspections. Even if he'd been caught red-handed at the scene of a murder, he'd still walk. The beauty of diplomatic immunity. He got up out of his first class seat and walked out into the terminal.

After passing through immigration with no problems, he saw his liaison, Hiram Jarrum, wave to him. He motioned him to silence and followed him out into the airport parking lot where they both got into the gold Jaguar.

"Have you found the answers I asked you for?" Ignacio said, coming directly to the point. "I understand we may have very little time until the girl leaves for the United States."

"Yes." Hiram replied. "As you have suspected, the plans to rebuild the temple have garnered tremendous support since the discovery of the Ark."

"Then it must be destroyed." Ignacio said. "This city is the place of Jesus, the son of our beloved Virgin Mary, we cannot permit the Jewish religion to return to it's former splendor by rebuilding their temple."

"I knew you would feel that way and I have already anticipated your request. Allow me to show you the plans I have made."

Hiram, half Jew and half Lebanese, was loyal to no one except his pocketbook and he was well paid by Ignacio to be his eyes and ears in the Holy Land. He drove the car through the back street past the Via Dolorosa, down a small cobblestone road past several vegetable carts and merchants selling olive wood statues, into an open courtyard. They got out of the car and went up the stairs where Hiram took a large key from his key chain and opened a medieval lock that resisted, but slowly gave way to the huge key. It took an effort from the small man to push the door open and they stepped into the dark. A young boy, Thomas, was sleeping by a large wooden crate. Hiram kicked him awake. He got up as if he were a maltreated animal and groveled before Hiram.

"Open the shutters Thomas and fetch some wine for our guest."

Hiram commanded, enjoying the subservience as one does who enjoys the raw nature of cruelty.

"Excuse me." Hiram said. "I found him when he was abandoned at a Palestinian camp nearly a year ago. He was going through my trunk, now as you can see he's..."

Ignacio interrupted, "He's your servant. Very wise. Now the suspense...it's a nice touch, but you didn't bring me up here to see your servant, now did you?"

Ignacio had a chilling way of questioning Hiram and it immediately brought the conversation back to its center.

"Over here." Hiram said from the window. "That's the museum where they are keeping the Ark." Hiram reached in his shirt and took off a key from a small string around his neck.

"Here, open that box. I think you'll be satisfied that the arrangements are complete."

Ignacio took the key looking at Hiram's foolish grin not giving him the satisfaction at smiling back. He walked over to the crate and opened it. He removed the plastic cover and looked at the SAM rocket launcher. He lifted it out and saw the eight rockets. He was impressed.

"Don't even ask me how I got it," Hiram stated, "but it can't be traced to here. It was brought in through the Golan. It's quite effective and from this distance remarkably accurate. A few well placed missiles and that building will be a mound of rubble. All that will remain of the Ark will be a mass of molten gold, indistinguishable from the other artifacts."

"One of the most extensive collections of Jewish art in the world." Ignacio thought as his mind was racing with hatred, "Destroyed as well."

Ignacio knew he'd have to destroy the man and the boy after the attack. No one could know that the church was behind an attack of this magnitude. He turned with a smile.

"You will be richly rewarded. You have indeed done well. We shouldn't waste any time. Who knows where they will be moving it too."

Ignacio went down to the Jaguar and looked around. He took out his briefcase and slipped his gun underneath his belt. He couldn't see Thomas looking at him from the window. Thomas had a sixth sense. Anyone who had to grow up on the streets learned to trust no one and suspect the worst from everyone. Thomas knew that those who carried guns had no reservation about using them.

When Ignacio went back into the room, he found a small feast set up before him. Grapes, oranges, cracker bread, cheeses and a cool yogurt with strawberries. The wine was in a large goblet and Ignacio was tired and jet-lagged. He took a long gulp. Thomas watched him warily. The launcher was laid out on the large refractory table. Ignacio studied it and within moments knew exactly how it worked. He also knew that although they had time to fire off several shots, the escape time had to be very quick. Israelis were under full alert at all time. It was a country where everyone always anticipated danger and hostilities and the response time was extremely rapid.

Mishi Ronan, the daughter of a Jewish emigrant from Odessa, walked by the plexiglass case containing the Ark. The years of oppression had left her cold to the love of God, but the Ark had began to effect her as it had affected everyone who came anywhere near it. She felt strangely alive and yet vulnerable to the immense power that emanated from it. Scriptures that she had never thought about in years ran through her mind as if she was hearing them for the first time. She thought about the way that she had been protected while stationed in the Sinai and how the supply truck laden with explosives had blown up and left her unharmed. The words of the ninety first Psalm came to her. "He shall give His angels charge over thee and you shall not be afraid of the arrows that fly by night." She wondered how her people could have so often taken for granted the protection of their God and knew she never would again. The light went black and she heard a huge explosion. Part of the ceiling started falling towards her. A chunk of plaster weighing over ten kilos hit her on her head and she went unconscious.

Ignacio loaded up another round and fired again seeing that his first one had scored a direct hit on the west wing. The next round tore into the large arched windows and blasted out the back. The third hit brought down the steel support that kept the roof intact. Ignacio watched as the building started to collapse. He loaded another missile and fired into the crumbling structure. The explosions were deafening. All around the Ark, precious art works were being decimated.

Within moments the Israeli counter-terrorist forces were converging on the area lead by Colonel Jonathan Netanyahu. Though unable to clearly pinpoint where the missile strikes were coming from, they were intent on neutralizing them.

Ignacio loaded up another round and sent it into the debris. He knew time was out. He turned to Hiram with his pistol.

Hiram's eyes opened in terror. "But my reward."

"You shall have your reward, but it is God who will give it to you." Ignacio's eye darted about for the boy before he pulled the trigger. Thomas was no where to be found. He had hid himself in a large trunk and was watching from the keyhole. Ignacio made an unsuccessful sweep of the room and gave up, quickly taking the keys of the car from Hiram. He ran downstairs and started the car. The streets were jammed with people who had heard the explosions and Ignacio was honking his horn trying desperately to get them out of the way before being cordoned off. It was hopeless. He was deadlocked. Ignacio abandoned the car and grabbed his briefcase forgetting his long overcoat in his haste to get out of the car. The sea of people was heading toward the explosions. Everyone had dreaded the worst. Ignacio had to claw his way over people to get away and had to slip into an empty doorway when he saw a troop of full dressed troops with Galil assault rifles approaching.

He stopped at a public rest room and cleaned himself off and went to the King David hotel where he had a regular suite. They checked him in without question and he turned on the evening news.

Reporters were on hand recording the scene. The grief on the faces of those looking on was incomprehensible. People were fainting at the horror of the very act. Many people had come down with shovels and the troops were coordinating the rescue efforts. It was an outrage of international proportions. Ignacio watched the body of Hiram being brought down the stairs and saw the soldiers hold onto a struggling Thomas. He murmured to himself about loose ends and realized that he'd have to quickly change his appearance and get out of the country. Within moments his beard was shaved and he had blonde hair. He burnt his passport and all identification papers, his clothes he wrapped in plastic and went downstairs and threw them in the dumpster. He had left himself a back door through Jordan. Within three hours he was out of the country.

The police discovered the abandoned Jaguar, jacket and had begun to put the pieces of the puzzle together. In the coat pocket was a stub with his seat number on. They were able to trace that as well. The young boy had a very good memory of faces and was able to give such a detailed description that you would have thought the police artists had sketched the face from a life model.

The trail lead back to the Vatican, but no one would comment. The funds for the ticket were Vatican funds, but no one would claim any recognition of the face though he was known to more than a few of them. Volturo was loose and no one knew where.

The Ark had mysteriously survived. The beams had come down around it, but it had remained undamaged as had Mishi who recovered after her mild concussion.

Julie and Ben rushed down to the major's office where the Ark had been taken for safekeeping. It was in a huge steel vault where all the documents were kept. Security was tight and it took them awhile to get through. When they finally did they were surprised to see the Ark in the same condition in which they had found it. The only difference was in the darkened vault, it was giving off a translucent glow.

The mayor's aide approached them. "As you see it has not been damaged. It's a miracle. The entire west wing of the museum is destroyed. Who would do such a thing?"

"Or why?" Ben answered. "We're leaving. Please have the priests remove the tablets and place them in this box."

Ben showed him the gold box that he had the jeweler make to transport the stone fragments back to America with. "We can't risk leaving this here any longer. You understand of course, when the temple is completed it will be returned and the amount of materials that we will be analyzing will be minute compared to the mass of the items to be examined."

"Of course," the assistant responded. "Several of the rabbis are here right now. I will do as you request."

While Ben and Julie stood by, the rabbis sanctified themselves and lifted the lid of the Ark. Inside they took the stone tablets and a piece from the original commandments that Moses in anger had smashed on the bottom of Mt. Sinai after witnessing the Israelites who had fallen into adultery. The transfer was made without incident and the box was handed to Ben. He turned to find Wilbur Tonney standing by five heavy set men in suits.

"There's a limo outside and a plane waiting. We've already taken the liberty of packing your bags. I suggest we make haste," Wilbur commanded.

Within minutes they were leaving Jerusalem and heading for the institute in Detroit. As Julie sat back on the plane, she looked out the window into the night sky and wondered why a God that was so amazing to have created the heavens and the earth cared so much for each individual. She snuck a look over at Ben and marveled how much he had changed in such a short time. He had gone from a cocky self-assured individual to someone who revered his Creator. She wondered if her proof was really going to mean anything to those who had purposed their hearts to remain agnostic no matter what the facts. It didn't matter to her whether or not anyone believed her, she only cared that they believed in God and their souls would be saved from eternal damnation. The thought of another human being spending eternity away from the love of God and suffering in a Hell hole was enough to drive her to tears. She reflected on her life and her years of rebellion and was thankful that God had mercy on her, she wished the same for others as well. She drifted off to sleep.

The Detroit Free Press sold more papers with Julie and Ben's picture on front than they had since the Kennedy Assassination. With exclusive interviews with Julie's parents, teachers, women group friends, they had managed to fill up the entire "A" section with her exploits making her a hero.

Her father had wasted no time in lining up additional testing equipment for the laboratory. He was able to secure some additional spectrometers and Harris Technical Services supplied him with their latest in laser imaging machines. It was so accurate that it was able to see things on an atomic level and would analyze the tablets with greater accuracy than had ever been possible. The National Science Foundation to whom Ford Motors had been a huge contributor was generous enough to help underwrite the ten million dollar machine cost.

The Guggenheim Foundation had been besieged with applications from all over the world, from the world's most eminent scientists who wanted to study the tablets and the Ark as well. The director could not even keep up with the volume of mail. The entire staff room was full of boxes of unopened mail. He decided to let Julie decide who she wanted to work with.

The plane landed at eight o'clock in the morning. Evidently the word had leaked out. The airport was swarming with television crews and photographers. The governor was there with a long stretch limousine and the elite of the Michigan State Police Riot squad. They had heard of the attempt in Israel to destroy the Ark and the bomb squad was along for good measure as well as an armored vehicle to transport the Ark to the safety of the laboratory which had been thoroughly combed for explosives. Lornell Fitzsimmons was no stranger to terrorists and was going to make sure that if anything happened to the Ark and its contents, it wasn't going to happen on his shift. No one knew the box they were bringing back with them was not the Ark. Ben had decided a diversion was best to throw the terrorists off the track.

Julie's mom and dad were escorted to the front and were the first to be seen by Julie when she descended the steps from the plane. She ran down into their arms and comforted her mom who was crying with grief and joy.

"Mom," Julie said. "I'm so sorry about Doug."

"Well," her mom replied. "At least you are back with us and we didn't lose both of you."

Before her mom could finish, Ben was looking at her with eyes full of compassion. He reached over and hugged her.

"Your son was a very brave man," Ben said. "You should be proud of him." Turning his attention to Julie's father, he continued. "Mr. Reinhold, I believe there's a hope we will all see Doug some day."

John's face beamed. "I believe that too, son. Well, I think we'd better get you over to the press conference. It appears the whole city has turned out to welcome you two."

CHAPTER TWELVE
Clouds of Glory

The Guggenheim Science Research Center adjoined the Worldwide Outreach Center. The city had donated the additional land, and the money to build the state of the art facility had come mostly from large corporate donors. They had done revolutionary work in the discovery of subatomic particle research. Now they were the center of worldwide attention as they attempted to unlock the secrets of the Ten Commandments. Jumpin' Jack had gone on nationwide television and invited anyone who wanted to see the Ten Commandments to come.

There were lines around the block and t-shirts with inscriptions like 'Ten Commandments -if you've broken one you've broken all' and 'Ten Commandments -Not Suggestions' sold along with posters, key chains and myriads of other items to the visitors who could view the video documentary put together to show the discovery. Refreshments booths were also set up and visitors were treated to free drinks and healthy snacks. It was the biggest event to hit Detroit since the invention of the automobile and people had driven from all over the country to see it.

Julie and Ben, worn out from their many interviews, sat outside on the balcony overlooking the crowd, drinking ice tea. Jumpin' Jack walked out, full of exuberance.

"Praise the Lord for bringing you two safely back from Ethiopia and Israel. I understand you went through some pretty harrowing experiences."

"More than harrowing" Ben commented. "We're lucky we didn't end up like Doug. What was it you wanted to talk to us about. Can I call you Jack?"

"Yes." Jack smiled. "Just not jackass. Least not to my face."

Ben missed the joke. Julie was too tired to react.

"When is Gale coming to join us?" Ben asked.

"She should be here in a few moments. I wanted to talk to you about your project. I admit I'm not much of a scientist though I know there are a lot of folks that find plenty of science in the Bible. I guess I'm just not educated enough to see it. I know that God was in the beginning and He made everything. I believe it and I believe in Jesus but I'd like to know, because a lot of people have been asking me, just what it is you are trying to prove? Because if it's a worthy cause I'm behind you all the way."

"Thanks for the support." Ben responded. "I'm an archaeologist just like Doug was. We go on digs and try to find out about the past piece by piece, fragment by fragment. We rummage through old garbage dumps, bones, rubble and try to determine what our ancestors were all about. Most of the time we use carbon dating to find out ages of things. From what I understand Julie's got something much different in mind."

"I do." Julie breathed in deeply centering her thoughts. "I'd like to show the world conclusively that these tablets can only have been written by the hand of God and contain the very voice of God."

"But how can you find the voice of God out of a stone tablet?" Jack questioned.

"I don't know for sure what is going to work but we're going to analyze the indentations on the stone as well and try and figure out how they got there."

"Well." Jack responded. "Looks like Gale probably got caught up in traffic. I'll call her on her cell phone and arrange for all of us to have lunch at Huggs. Does that sound OK with you two?"

"Is it kosher?" Ben asked

"Is he serious?" Jack retorted to Julie. "Well, let's put it this way. This place is so clean you could eat off the floors and they don't serve ham and eggs."

"Then it's fine with me. "Ben replied. "But I was really hoping for pigs in the blanket."

Jack got the joke and shared a good laugh with him. The ice was broken and he knew he could be himself.

The restaurant was on top of the Renaissance Towers, a luxury development right in the heart of decaying Detroit. It was a monolith to the transportation giants that had brought commerce and prosperity to the city only to abandon it for the promise of safe, comfortable suburban living. They were promptly seated and Julie was buried in the menu when she felt a tap on her shoulder. She looked up into the face of her ex-fiance Tim. Her face turned ash-white.

"Welcome back" Tim spoke. "You're a celebrity now.

Congratulations."

"I'm enjoying my few moments in the limelight." She jested. "Tim, you know Pastor Wallace and his wife Gale."

"Yes." Tim responded eyeing Ben. He placed his hand on her shoulder in a familiar way and challenged Ben.

Ben got up angry and flattened Tim with one round house punch to the temple that sent him sprawling back into a serving cart.

"I suggest you keep your hands to yourself Pretty boy. Unless you want some more of where that came from."

Tim brushed off his jacket and got up pretending to ignore Ben.

"No Jew kike is going to push me around. Go back to your stinking desert."

Tim took a wild punch and connected on Ben's ear throwing him into the waiter carrying a full tray of deserts. Two husky men got up to join Tim. One of them grabbed Ben and held him so Tim could take a free shot. Jack was too fast. he got up out of his seat, grabbed the big man's arm and twisted it back. Ben was able to regain his footing and slip away, but before he could move completely to the side the other man dressed in a navy blue business suit elbowed him squarely across the mouth breaking out his front tooth, splattering blood everywhere. Jack bounded over and lifted the other man off of Ben and threw him into the grand piano. The piano's legs split under the impact and the entire piano came down on the man's leg.

"Help me. "The man cried. "Get this thing off me. It's breaking my leg."

Everyone came to their senses and Jack in a show of superhuman strength lifted up the piano while Ben dragged the man out from under it. Security guards who had been called by the day manager came in as well as Metro Police and paramedics. They quickly separated the quarrelling parties and started treating the cuts and bruises. After fifteen minutes of questioning and a thousand dollar check from Jack. The four left under a flurry of flashbulbs.

"We'd better get you to a dentist." Jack said looking in his rear view mirror at Ben. "You need to keep that temper down. A few more antics like that and we're going to have to graze at drive-in's only."

"Very funny honey. " Gale said sharply. "But if you ask me. I think Ben was doing the right thing. I didn't see any reason for Tim to have his hands on Julie. It showed a total lack of respect."

"You're right." Jack answered. "If someone had laid there hands on you I probably would have them around a pole like a pretzel. It just bothers me to have to pay a thousand dollars for damages to that old piano. People are really going to think I'm crazy now."

"You never cared before what people thought?" Julie said. "Why care now?"

Julie found herself with a new respect for Ben. Not only did he respect and honor her, he expected others to do it as well. She shivered at the thought of spending her life with a man that loved her like that. She wasn't a violent person, but inside she was glad that Ben had knocked Tim down. "It served him right." She thought to herself.

Leroy Underwood grew up by the Detroit River. His father, when he was alive, had worked for the Chevrolet plant until he was hit by a crane that had sent him head first into a plume of hot steel. There was nothing remaining of his body to be buried and Leroy grew up wondering what his father would have thought of him. His mother was an industrious sort. She did her best to keep him and his three sisters out of trouble. She took the transit bus to the suburbs every day working as a cleaning lady. Leroy dreamed of playing professional baseball for the Detroit Tigers but had no acumen for the sport. He couldn't hit to save his life and his fielding was so bad his teammates had nicknamed him "Butter." They teased him mercilessly until one day his eighth grade science

The Voice

teacher, Jonathan Kersey, graduate of Howard University, had found him under the stairwell crying. From that day on, Leroy had a mentor. Jonathan watched over Leroy like he was his older brother. It wasn't long before Leroy was winning prizes in school-sponsored science projects and the same friends that had called him Butter were calling him Professor and asking him for help with their homework. He finished his high school science classes his sophomore year and began taking entry level college classes in science and physics. When he graduated, to his mother's joy, he had earned a full-ride scholarship to Michigan State in Lansing. He was devoted to the study of the atom and had developed his own computer programs using them to analyze the plethora of data available to him through the University's well-endowed science facility. Instruments beyond the budgets of entire third world countries were at his fingertips pointing him to a world far removed from the visible spectrum of experience. He was searching for the very essence of life itself in subatomic particles.

He had earned his masters in a record three years and by the time he was twenty-three had earned a doctorate as well. The Guggenheim Foundation had given him a grant for his study of subatomic particles and he was among those credited with finding and documenting smaller particles than the atom. Because of his strong upbringing in the Pentecostal Free Church he found himself constantly at odds with the heads of various departments who in spite of massive amounts of information pointing to a Creator were avowed evolutionists. Shortly after graduation he moved back to Detroit to finish his grant out with the Guggenheim Foundation. He had never dreamed that someday the original Ten Commandments would be put in front of him and the responsibility for analyzing them for a skeptical world would fall on his shoulders.

After receiving the additional equipment he needed to professionally do his study, he ran a program sampling rock that was bombarded with lasers. He began to develop the most complete study of how the molecular and atomic nature of rock changed under intense heat. When he finally got his chance to chip off small pieces of the tablets, directly in the areas that had been carved in, he was ready. His initial analysis gave him a reading similar to the molecular breakdown of the volcanic lava which was thousands of degrees centigrade of hot rock that he had himself bombarded with heavy doses of laser-directed radiation. There was a marked difference between the area that had been scooped out and the surrounding stone. He could find no trace of any metal from a carving instrument used to scoop out the letters. The discovery led him to believe that there was no chisel used on the tablets. He ran to the adjoining laboratory to report his findings to Julie.

"Julie. " He said barely bothering to knock. "I've got some good news and I've got some better news. Which would you like to hear first?"

"The better. " She said smiling enjoying his constant sense of humor. "But before you start yourself, I want you to know that the program you invented for the audio sampling is awesome. Unless there's a change in polarity it seems like rocks can hold sound waves indefinitely."

"Well," He grabbed her arm. "I insist you follow me and see some things firsthand.

Within moments she understood his analysis and was exuberant.

"It's too early to publish." She gushed. "But it really is wonderful. I can't wait to tell Dr. Gibron."

"Julie," Leroy responded. "While you were out with Dr. Gibron last night, I did some more tests on our rock samples. I don't see any way to gradiate the time-domain of the stored signals especially using the spectral method like we are that covers all the frequencies."

"What are you saying?" Julie said a little distressed that bad news was following up the good news.

"We need a sampling of God's voice, the frequencies, and we need to run a tracking on that. Otherwise we have found a thousand years of sound on those tablets. We'd need so many megabites and gigabites and thousands of technicians to listen to the playback and try and determine which sounds were just random and which are defined speech patterns." Leroy studied her for her reaction.

"That's all Dr. Underwood?" She said thinking. "If that's the only problem then I guess we'll just have to get a bigger computer. We'll make a sample of someone reading the Ten Commandments in the ancient Hebrew language and if we need a thousand people to analyze the data or however many, we'll just get another computer and program it to do the work."

"In other words."

"Yes." Julie smirked. "Congratulations on your last success. Now, would you please start working on a program to eliminate common sounds such as lightning, thunder, wind, crowd noise and work on a program to pull out that specific sound when the Lord God appeared to Moses and gave him these tablets."

"Yes." Leroy responded his face breaking into a big grin. "Yes Dr. Reinhold, sir, I mean, ma'm. I'll get right on it."

Ignacio had surfaced in Istanbul and gone overland back to Rome. There in a quiet suburb he kept a safe house under a different identity known to no one. He was furious that the Ark had survived the attack and wondered if he was fighting against God in a battle he had no chance of winning. He shook off the thought and decided it would be best to destroy all the evidence that the Ark and it's contents were authentic. He turned his attention to the Guggenheim Research Center where, according to well publicized information, the Ark had been taken. He was sure that the contents of the Ark were kept several places and he knew that his mission was not going to be a simple one. He was no scientist but he understood computers. He decided the best way to discredit the findings was to have a virus placed in the computer system that would disrupt and alter the data to make it indecipherable. By noon the next day he was on Air Italia flying to Boston to meet with Jack Dunlop, a man that specialized in industrial espionage, and a man who for the right price could get into any system anywhere.

He cleared U.S. Customs with barely a three minute delay. He had decided to leave all of his personal armaments behind and buy whatever he needed stateside. He knew that if the computer virus didn't work he would just systematically eliminate those working on the project. One way or another the world was not going to be given the proof that the Ark was the real thing. He took a cab downtown to the Hilton and after checking in went straight to his room. He knew the authorities had connected him to the bombing of the museum and decided after looking in the mirror to go even farther with his disguise. He had picked up a flowing orange robe and decided to shave his balding head completely and don the clothes of a Buddhist Monk. After nicking his head several times He looked at his new persona and smiled -The Happy Buddha.

His meeting with Jack Dunlop took place in a small park near the Boston Art Museum.

"I trust you have my fee?" Jack said glancing down at the shoulder bag Ignacio was carrying.

"Yes." Ignacio replied. "You are certain you can penetrate the security system at the Guggenheim?"

"Never been there." Jack replied nonchalantly. "But I've been to Detroit dozens of times. the Japanese are always anxious to know what New American styles are coming out."

Ignacio thought, then handed him the shoulder bag. "I'll be in Detroit at the Renaissance Center. You won't recognize me but I'll contact you."

Unknown to both parties a surveillance camera hundreds of yard away was recording their meeting. The trails that Jack had left behind him after many of his jobs were often sloppy and NSA had finally caught up with him and had him under full investigation for industrial espionage."

Jack got in his car and drove back to his posh brownstone and opened the suitcase. it contained over two hundred thousand dollars of brand new currency. He was tired of the exchange in Hong Kong and was glad he wasn't going to have to launder the money. He walked into the library and pushed a paneled door open. Behind the door he had another panel that unscrewed. He took it off and placed the contents into the safe. He had already done some preliminary checking into the Guggenheim. He was able to obtain copies of all their purchase orders and knew every piece of equipment that they had. He was amazed that their research department was so sophisticated, but he had run into many tough systems before and no encryption was going to keep him from doing what he needed to do. For a moment his conscience panged him. He wondered if it was right to keep the world from knowing whether the Ten Commandment were really given by God or not. He thought of the many he had broken. "Thou shalt not steal." That was how he made his living. "Keep Holy the Sabbath." He hadn't gone to church since his alcoholic father had died when he was sixteen, leaving him to care for their sickly mother and younger sister Grace. "Thou shalt not covet thy neighbor's goods." There wasn't anything he didn't want bigger or better than someone else. "Thou shalt not bear false witness against thy neighbor." He thought of all the phony identification cards and scams he had pulled to get into the various corporate headquarters he had raided. "Thou shalt not take the name of the Lord thy God in vain." To him the name of Jesus Christ was an expression just like some people said "Hell." "Honor thy Father and Thy Mother." That was a laugh, after his old man died he stuck around home until he was out of high school and then took off. He didn't know whether his aged mom was dead or alive. "Have no graven images before me." He thought about how he worshipped his Lexus. "Thou shalt not kill." He reflected about his dead child. Dead because he had callously told his girlfriend Trish to either get rid of it or he'd get rid of her. He was glad he didn't believe in a god because if he did, he knew God wasn't going to be very pleased with his life.

Jack's flight to Detroit was short and uneventful and while he was sleeping a dream kept coming to his mind. He was in a maze and was wandering from path to path each time running into another wall. He started running and tried to climb over but found the wall too slippery and too tall. It began to storm and lightning bolts came down breaking up sections of the wall. Right in front of him an entire section of the wall collapsed and he felt a hand take his and guide him over the rubble. When he got out he found himself in a wide open field full of flowers with children running about and singing.

"Is this Heaven?" He had asked the young child standing next to him.

"No Dad." The young boy replied. "It's not. Heaven's up there. We don't know if we get to go or not. We were never born."

The dream shook his spirit and he awoke abruptly just as the stewardess was passing by.

"We're going to be landing shortly. Please fasten your safety belt." She said.

He did so, but remained fast asleep.

A few minutes later the flight attendant was shaking his shoulder. He looked up at the name tag. It read, "Holli."

"Sir." She exclaimed. "We've landed. The cleaning crew's on their way in. You're going to need to deplane."

"Sure." Jack said, studying her. "Say, would you consider having a drink with me, that is, if you're done with your flights for the evening."

She looked him over. "Just a drink, nothing else?"

"Yeah." Jack responded. "Just a drink. Where are you staying?"

"We stay in the Renaissance Center."

"Great then." Jack got up. "How about the lobby bar in about an hour."

"Sure." Holli replied. "What's your name?"

"Jack."

Back in Washington the NSA was pouring over the picture of Jack and the Buddhist Monk.

"Whoever this guy is that Jack Dunlop is talking to is obviously wearing a disguise. You can see the tan lines where his head has been recently shaved. Can we do a facial analysis and tray to match something from our files?" Agent Clarence Stewart spoke. "Something's not right about these two."

"Sir." The young assistant, Ted Cox, replied. "Why don't we just bring him in now. We've got more than enough to string him up."

"Theodore." The commander answered. "Oftentimes when the fly is in the web, the spider plays with it and waits to attract others. Let's see what our bait brings in."

The computer programmer was able to enhance the photo of Ignacio. Specific readings were made of his facial structure. Hundreds of calculations were made by the visual imaging program from every possible angle. Although picture and prints of known terrorists were stored in the mainframe data base, it took the computer programmer hours to run through the entire lists. The results were nil. When Ted returned to the Commander's office. He nearly ran into Wilbur Tonney on his way out. The folder with the papers spilled out all over the floor, including the fully enhanced color image of Ignacio. Wilbur bent down and picked it up.

"Looks familiar." Wilbur said, studying the picture. "Is he one of your operatives?"

"No." Clarence said, looking up from his desk at the image Wilbur was holding. We've been trying to place him. We caught him on film at the Boston Art Museum talking to one of our perps. They exchanged what appeared to be quite a bundle."

"No." Wilbur thought aloud. "It couldn't be related."

"What?" Clarence was stumped.

"Let me hang on to this photo." Wilbur said. "I've got to get back to Detroit. I'll call you from there."

One of the perks of the assignment, Operation Moses as they called it, was the use of a private jet. Ninety minutes later he was back in Detroit and at the Guggenheim meeting with Julie and Ben.

The Voice

The room was decorated with plush black leather furniture and Chagall lithos. Ben and Leroy were at the table with Dr. Anderson the President of the Institute.

"Good evening Ms. Reinhold." Dr Anderson addressed her. "I believe you know Mr. Tonney."

"Yes." Julie responded. "He was kind enough to offer us our escort from Jerusalem. Thank you again. But I'm sure you didn't bring me out of the gym for chit-chat. What's on your mind?"

" It's not customary for us to reveal investigations to those in the civilian sector." Wilbur injected. "But given the nature of the sensitive assignment you're all working on and it's possible global implications, I think it's appropriate for me to break protocol."

He pulled out a picture of Ignacio from Interpol and the photo of the Buddhist Monk and slid them across the table.

"This man is a Vatican Emissary Ignacio Robella, forty-three years old. A sworn defender of the faith. He operates with complete autonomy, creates his own agenda and lets nothing get in the way of accomplishing it. All is justified in his mind if he believes it represents the best interests of the Holy Mother Church."

"What are you saying? Why show us his picture? What does it have to do with our work here? Surely it's in the interest of the Roman Church that we prove these tablets are real." Ben stated.

"Well." Wilbur clarified. "It would seem so, but for some reason he recently hired one of the best men in the Western Hemisphere and sent him to Detroit for computer espionage. Although we can't place him directly at the scene in Jerusalem. One of his fingerprints was identified on the rocket launcher. It was a partial but an exact match."

"Great." Leroy rubbed his chin. "Where is he now? We've got a lot of information stored on hard drive. We're totally susceptible to off line penetration. We're not running a very complex encrypted system. This is a scientific investigation. It wouldn't take an Einstein to break in and tamper with or destroy our data."

"Then I suggest you make it tamper proof and quickly"

"Excuse me Mr. Tonney." Dr. Anderson spoke, drawing a bead of smoke out of his pipe. "Just what type of danger does this man represent to the Institute? We don't have the actual Ark, just the tablets."

"I know what he's after." Julie thought coolly. "Since he couldn't destroy the Ark, then he's determined to destroy our authentication process so the skeptics can dismiss us as hucksters."

"Precisely." Wilbur answered. "If he can't destroy your research then he'll attempt to destroy all of you. Any way you look at it we're not taking any needless chances. All of you are being assigned twenty-four hour protection. When you eat, when you sleep they'll be your shadows."

"Just how good is this espionage fellow?" Leroy queried.

"Real good. He just got a little overconfident and left some trails behind." Wilbur ended.

Fortunately for the Institute, Jack was enjoying a scenic diversion with the flight attendant he had shared drinks with. Holli was on a two day layover and they had enjoyed each other's company so much she had agreed to go to Grand Island for the day with Jack. She wondered about him and was enchanted by the mystery man behind the dark sunglasses. She found he was a contented listener and gave very few insights into his life or career.

"We're not allowed to take the car on the ferry." She said as they pulled up. "This island is for bikes and horses only."

"How charming." Jack answered. "The whole world would be out of work if everyone thought like that. But who knows, after months in Boston, Tokyo and Los Angeles I might get used to some fresh air."

"Let's go." Holli said, grabbing her daytime bag. "The ferry looks like it's filling up fast."

They were the last two on and barely edged by the ticket taker roping off the gangway. They rushed up holding hands. A tinge of guilt flowed over Holli. She had made a promise to God she wouldn't date anyone out of her faith and here she was already holding hands with someone she virtually knew nothing about. She resolved to interrogate him and find out his beliefs. She pulled her small Bible out of her purse as they sat in a bench seat on the bow.

"What's that?" Jack questioned.

"My Bible." Holli replied. "I always try to read it at the start of every day. How about you? Do you have one?"

"Yea. " Jack answered. "I collect old books. I've got a few old leather bound ones. One cost me nearly fifty thousand dollars. Did you know that the original Guttenberg Bible is priceless. It's the first book to ever roll off the printing press."

"No. I didn't. But I'm glad they're a lot cheaper to come by now. Otherwise who would ever be able to afford them? This one was given by the Gideons when I enrolled in college. I've had it ever since."

Jack looked at the well worn book. "It looks pretty worn out. You must be pretty serious about it. You really believe it was written by God?"

"Yes." Holli said. "I really do. The words in it change me a little more every time I read them. But I don't just read them. I mediate on them. It's awesome. Here let me read you my favorite Psalm. They were old song lyrics, many of them written by King David. He's the shepherd boy that killed Goliath the giant with a slingshot. Here's my favorite. Psalm fifteen. 'Who may enter my temple? Just those whose words are true and sincere and do no harm to their neighbor.' The psalmist is telling us that to enter the presence of God we have to be totally honest and free from all sins."

"Why do we need to be honest?" Jack reasoned. "Isn't God supposed to know everything anyways?"

"Yes." Holli smiled. "That's just the point. God wants us to be honest with ourselves. We know instinctively what is right and wrong. I mean we lie to someone and immediately we justify ourselves with this great sounding excuse. Almost as smooth as an argument delivered by F. Lee Bailey, the famous trial attorney. We get ourselves off with our own lies. But don't you see, Jack? We are just living in that lie. God knows all about our excuses. He wants our words, our thoughts to be true and sincere. He says. 'Come let us reason together. Though your sins be as scarlet, I will make them as white as snow. I'll take your sins and throw them into the sea of forgetfulness. I won't look at them anymore.' God alone has the power to make our sins disappear. It's His choice and something he loves to do; but, we've got to be brutally honest with Him and quit hiding behind our own lies, blaming others for the way we are, or our circumstances."

"In other words." Jack reiterated. "We've got to come clean. It sounds easy Holli, but maybe it's not for everybody -- there was a saying in my house. When my dad would come home drunk and pass out on the couch, my mom used to say, 'Let the sleeping dog lie.' Why wake something up that's just going to cause you trouble?"

"Is that what you want to do with your conscience? Just let it stay sleeping?" She probed. "Don't you know it's your guide through life? If you listen to it you won't have to spend eternity separated from God. Let it take you into a right standing relationship with God. When it's clear, you won't have anything to fear from God and no reason to hide."

"Do you remember when Adam and Eve sinned?" Holli asked. "Afterwards they hid themselves from God's presence."

"I remember they wore fig leaves." Jack said. "I don't remember they hid."

"That's what you are doing. You don't want to face the consequences of your sins, your choices to do what you wanted to do even when those choices violated your own sense of right and wrong. So now, you hide. by covering your sins with lies, excuses. You probably compare yourself to others you think are much worse than you - maybe your alcoholic father. You excuse your own sins because someone else is worse. That's not how it works with God. We've all got to stand in His light, in His presence. We can't be making excuses and hiding behind our lies. The truth will come out then. It's much easier to get it out now while you can still do something about the consequences."

"Why?" Jack thought aloud, wondering how he could change his entire criminal career. "It's all pretty relative. I don't hurt anybody. I do what I need to get by. I go my own way. I haven't hurt you have I?"

"No Jack." Holli said sadly. "Eventually you will. You can't help it. Either you serve God consciously or you serve yourself and Satan unconsciously."

"I don't even believe in Satan." Jack explained.

"Not believing in him is not going to make him disappear. In fact he's glad most people don't believe in him. Very few are going to openly embrace evil. Most people are going to do what you do - hide behind thin veneers of self-righteousness. How about it Jack? Are you going to play right into his hands believing he doesn't exist?"

They passed the rest of the trip in silence and got off on Grand Island and rented a tandem bike. They took an exhilarating ride down to the old Grand Hotel and went in for lunch. Jack was in awe of the place.

"This place is great. How long have you been coming here?" He asked

"My folks used to take us here every summer to visit my grandmother. She'd rent a room for the whole month of August. My sister and I always used to stay behind for a few extra days."

"Where are your parents now?" Jack questioned.

"My dad retired from General Motors and my mom runs an Antique Mall over by Dearborn. They like the life, attending auctions, going to estate sales, flea markets. I've got half my furniture from them, How about yours?"

"I haven't seen my mom in ages and quite honestly I'm not even sure she's alive. My dad's dead. No great loss to the world."

The Voice

Unbeknownst to anyone, Julie and Ben had snuck away for a trip up to Grand Island. Ben had been wanting to get her away and they had given their assigned bodyguard the slip and figured no one would follow them up to the remote island.

Julie was shocked to look up and see Holli.

"Holli." She exclaimed.

"Jules." Holli replied, going over to them at their table. " Of all the places. I read about Doug. I'm so sorry."

"Thanks. "Julie said, shaking her hand." Holli, this is my fiance Ben Gibron. Dr."

"Nice to meet you." Holli said, feeling awkward about introducing Jack.

"Who's your friend?" Julie asked. "Are you going to introduce us? You're not engaged too are you?"

"I'm Jack." He said extending his hand. "We just met, I was on her flight. She was nice enough to show me around. Excuse me a minute I'm going to wash up before lunch. Nice meeting both of you.'

While Jack was in the washroom, Holli continued chatting with Julie.

"Why don't you bring your new friend to church tomorrow? We have an early service and afterwards I can take you to the Institute and show you the Ten Commandments. They're amazing."

"That fellow you're with sure looks familiar." Ben added. "I swear I've seen him somewhere."

"There's our waiter coming with our food. I'll try to drag Jack along with me tomorrow. I can sense the Holy Spirit softening him up."

"Why did you say that? "Julie directed her comment at Ben.

"Nothing." He replied, watching Jack walk out of the men's room. "I just think I've seen him before."

"I have too." She said. "In a lot of movies. He looks like one of the Baldwin brothers. I hope Holli brings him tomorrow. She doesn't get to church much anymore with her airline job."

"Maybe she serves God outside the four walls of her church." Ben replied.

"She probably does but we still need to be plugged in where we can be regularly ministered to. I'm going to pray she comes to church tomorrow. We're going to have to get back before six. Maybe take an earlier ferry. I'm anxious to see what Leroy is doing with that new assignment I gave him."

"What?" Ben wondered.

"He's encrypting the Hebrew from the book of Exodus"

"There were a lot of phrases." Ben said, "The Lord gave specific commands for nearly every aspect of life. He knew none of us were capable of keeping all the commandments so He made provisions for us all"

"Ben, before we go back. I want to take you to visit a small cove I used to go to when I was a child. It's not too far. We can ride our bikes over."

Ben and Julie's movements were being carefully tracked by Ignacio who decided to step up his timetable. He was happy they had ditched their bodyguards. It made his job that much easier

They rode their bikes about ten minutes and parked them in a grove of trees. They climbed down using exposed roots as a type of ladder and walked out on the natural rock bridge in the lake.

"Ben took Julie in his arms and kissed her. "I can see why this place is special to you. It's beautiful."

"Yea." Julie nudged closer to him. "I used to come here all the time even at night and I'd sit and look at the stars and watch the water lap upon the rocks. Now it's even more special because you're here with me to share it."

Ignacio had followed them to the shore. While they were talking he had tried to get a clear shot but realized at the best he'd only kill one of them. He decided to immobilize them and go for a clear shot on the open road.

Ben looked at his watch and saw that it was nearly time for their ferry.

The Voice

"What time is it?" Julie asked.

"It's nearly six." Ben responded.

"We've got about fifteen minutes to get to the dock. the last ferry leaves at six twenty. If we don't get it we'll be stuck here all night."

They scrambled up as quickly as they could. Several times Julie nearly lost her grip but found the strong hands of Ben around her lifting her towards the top. They both rushed for their bikes and found the tires slashed. Ben instinctively grabbed Julie and pulled her aside. He motioned with his lips for her to keep quiet. They stealthily went through the narrow section of woods by the cliff.

"We'll have to get back to the hotel," Ben whispered. "Someone doesn't want us leaving here."

"Do you think it's that terrorist?" Julie questioned.

Ben unstrapped his small ankle holster and brandished his Bauer 25mm pistol.

"I think we're on our own. This won't help much but at least we're not defenseless."

Ignacio was watching through high powered infrared scopes. He was surprised to see them duck into the woods. He had the bike area pinned down and was hoping to take them both out. He had picked up a single shot Winchester 52D bolt action target rifle. He cursed its cumbersomeness and wished for his own gun. Without proper I.D. it was the best sniper piece he was able to buy. He had bought it from an unscrupulous pawn shop in Pontiac along with a Viola case.

No one had given second thought to a tuxedo dressed bald man carrying a large musical case. He cursed his misfortune and decided to take a shot and kill them one at a time. He took a bead on Ben's white jacket still visible slightly in the dusk. He aimed his sight low to allow for the recoil and squeezed. The bullet grazed Ben's shoulder and he slumped to the ground. He motioned Julie to keep moving. She stood frozen in fear like a deer caught in the headlight of a Mack truck.

"Ben!" She cried out. Another bullet dug into the tree next to her head.

"We're pinned down." Ben observed. "We've got to make some kind of diversion or he's just going to use us as target practice all night. I think the rifle fire is coming from over there." He pointed. "I saw the flash of the muzzle.

Ben pointed to a small patch of bushes on top of a knoll. "I'm going to try and get around him while you go off and get help."

"There IS no help." Julie said sadly. "The hotel has an old security guard who's about eighty. There's no police. This is a private island."

Ben looked up again. A bullet came whizzing by his head.

"He's got the range on me." He said. "My gun is like a pea shooter."

"God didn't bring us here to die like rabbits. Let's pray." Julie took his hands. "Lord, You said You'd send your angels to help us. You said in Psalm Ninety One You'd cover us with Your wings. Please Lord. We need your help now."

They both continued praying, offering no visible target to Ignacio. From over the lake a wind blew in dark clouds. The sky which had been growing darker with the descent of the sun began to grow black. Large drops of rain fell. The rain was so thick that visibility was reduced to zero. Ignacio realized it was futile to hunt them any longer. He cursed the darkness, left his bicycle and made his way back to the hotel. Before he got to the entrance. He hid his gun in the bushes by the side door and was dismayed to find it locked. He had to walk through the lobby in his mud streaked clothes. Several guests looked up at him aghast. He ignored them and went up the stairs to his room.

After waiting a while longer, Ben and Julie went back to the hotel using the woods for a partial cover. The rain continued to pour down until they were on the hotel grounds. The concierge saw the blood on Ben's jacket and called the Michigan State Police which sent over a chopper with a medic on board. The chopper flew them back to Detroit where they were greeted by Wilbur Tonney.

"I hope you two lovebirds check in with me before you go off on any more romantic interludes. Thank goodness whoever was shooting at you was only using twenty-two caliber ammunition. he must have been planning a clean shot to the heart. Look, I've checked your condition with the doctor. There is no need for you to remain here any longer. We want you both to stay with your parents. It's gated and it will be easier for my men to watch. No more running off, Okay?"

"I think I saw him." Julie said ignoring the request.

"Saw who?" Wilbur responded. Ben looked at her as well, a puzzled expression on his face.

"I saw Ignacio's head. It was white like he had recently shaved it. Does that help any?" She addressed Tonney for approval.

"Yea." Tonney responded. "We'll keep our eyes out for a balding priest."

"He wasn't dressed like a priest. I think I spotted him when we got off the ferry. He was wearing a tuxedo and carrying a viola case. Check it out with the hotel. He had to have checked in there."

"How would he even have known where we were going?" Ben asked. "We had barely decided ourselves,"

"Remember I called you on my cellular before I picked you up. Maybe he was following me and got me on a scanner."

"We'll check it out."

By the time they sent a team back to the hotel on Grand Island, Ignacio was gone. The clerk confirmed the description and even described him coming in covered with mud. A nearby homeowner had filed a report of a missing boat and Wilbur figured it had probably been stolen by Ignacio for his escape. Wilbur wondered how they'd ever trap someone so elusive.

That evening Ben was sitting talking with John Reinhold. they were both smoking big cigars to the dismay of the women. The pungent smell mixed well with the leather and old book smell of the

The Voice

Reinhold library.

"So," John continued. "How do you think the folks back in Israel will take the news of your conversion to Christianity?"

"I don't know." Ben thought seriously. "It seems like the most logical and natural decision I ever made. Why would this universe show such signs of intelligent life and so many people think that the very one who created us would not be interested in communicating with us? There's order in every strata of creation down to the smallest subatomic particles."

"What is it you two are trying to prove in your experiments? I'd like to help." John said.

"You already have, More than you know." Ben said with genuine admiration. "Getting your company to underwrite such a large portion of the Guggenheim Foundation. What more could we ask for?"

"I mean really help. Not just financially. "John added. "Front line. You bring me on the data and I'll be a spokesman for you two. Shield you from the crazies and make sure those who need to get to you can. How about it? I'm not afraid of dying. Been there already."

Ben stood and walked around and then back to John's rich leather chair. "You've got it. Come down to the Institute tomorrow. We'll be showing some people around. I'll show you in detail what we're trying to accomplish and then you can decide first hand if you really still want in."

All night John dreamt he was in the Institute and he could see the light emanating from the tablets. He faced an evil presence that was holding the tablets in the air. explosives were wired around his waist. He instinctively grabbed the tablets and wrestled them out of the creature's hands. He awoke in a cold sweat. Outside a night owl hooted and he went to the window. There below him he watched the agent patrolling the grounds. He went downstairs to further think about his dream. He knew instinctively a sinister force was preparing to destroy the Institute and if that happened, there was a good chance his daughter would die as well. Without second thought he dropped to his knees to pray.

Outside of the Renaissance Center Ignacio, dressed in plain business attire, but wearing a grey wig, paced back and forth. He had called and left several messages for Jack Dunlap and grew more and more irritated when none of them were returned. He had seen Jack with the girl and wanted to strangle him for mixing business with pleasure. There were several vows he had taken seriously, the first was to protect his church and the other was his vow of celibacy. He regarded others who had physical needs as being weak and lustful. He remembered the sounds of his parents making love through the thin walls of their seaside cottage. His portable phone rang.

"Hello." Jack spoke.

"I saw you today. Did you have a nice break lover boy?" Ignacio spewed out his venomous hatred through the receiver. "Now get yourself downstairs. We have some business to conclude."

Jack was freaked out. He had never had a client trail him. He was wondering if Ignacio was a psychopath. He put his shoes on and came down the elevator. Outside the streets were deserted. He saw the silhouette of Ignacio standing menacingly blowing cigarette rings.

"Smoke?" Ignacio having calmed down was like a different person smiling and offering him a cigarette.

Jack didn't want to offend him and responded. "No. It's bad for my lungs. What's the point of you following me around. You told me I had five days.

"Well. You've used up three. Already it might be too late. You don't understand. This information absolutely must not get out."

"Well." Jack retorted "Thanks to my messing around. I've now got a foolproof way of getting into the Institute. Once I get in I'll pretend I've got to leave and hide myself. I'm not going to have any trouble accessing the computer so I'll beat your original schedule. Not only that, tomorrow I get to see the tablets. You never told me why you are in a rush to get rid of them. I thought Catholics believed in the Ten Commandments."

"Yea." Ignacio coughed. "We believe in them. We've even added quite a few of our own. But if those things are proven beyond a shadow of a doubt to be the real thing then no one is going to dispute the Jew's rights to rebuild their temple. We dispute that right and I'm going to make damn sure it doesn't happen. What time do you think you'll be finished?"

We're going to the institute about noon. I'll slip away about one. I should have it all wrapped by five at the latest. Now I'm exhausted. Can I go back to bed?"

"Who's bed? Adulterers and whore mongers God will judge."

"The same bed I've slept in every night I've been here in the hotel by myself."

Jack was fed up. He turned and walked away and breathed a sigh of relief when he entered the glass door of the hotel. He was happy Ignacio hadn't dispatched him with a bullet in the back.

Ignacio got in his car and drove down to where a huge crater in the ground was being dug out for the World Wide Outreach Center indoor stadium. He had no trouble getting over the barbed wire fenced enclosure and within no time had found the main construction shack. He shot off the bulletproof padlock and went inside. He knew anything containing nitro was always stored on site, Nobody ever wanted to move it more than was necessary. He saw the box on the floor and tore it open. He placed eight sticks in the sacks and headed out. He walked a few steps and heard a distinctive growl followed by another. He was being tracked. The guard dogs were a Rotweiller and Siberian Wolf mix. He felt his heart pound as if it were a kettle drum beating out the end of the 1812 Overture. He picked up his pace and reached for his hand pistol. A shadow darted by and he took a shot. It went wild.

The dogs were hunting him as a prey. They were also very wary of humans, having been trained to trust only their master. Jaco, the oldest of the two, could smell the fear emanating from his sweat glands. He salivated and bounded up the huge pile of girders right over where Ignacio had hidden. Kindra, slightly smaller had gone around to flush him out.

Ignacio knew he was being cornered. He took a stick of explosives and broke it in two and rolled it on the ground next to him. He felt the wind grow warmer as Kindra's body drew close. There was no light and no reflection. Ignacio took a draw off his glowing cigarette and flicked it towards the explosive and ran. Jaws enclosed around his legs at the same time he heard a tremendous explosion. The huge pile of girders came down. he heard the terrified howl of Jaco being crushed under the steel girders. The grip around his leg grew momentarily weaker and Ignacio took his other foot giving the attacking dog a quick shot to the skull. The dog released it's grip yelping with pain.

Jaco had leaped off the pile but gotten pinned under one of the girders. The noise had awakened Dave Terry, the night watchman who ran over to investigate. He was too late. Ignacio was already over the fence and down the street.

Jumpin' Jack Wallace got a phone call about three in the morning from a Detroit Metro Police Officer.

"Who is it?" Gale said, still sleeping and reluctant to get out of bed.

"Police." Jack answered putting on his jogging sweats. "Break-in down at the construction site. Police want me down to answer some questions. Somebody helped themselves to some rather powerful explosives."

"What about Dave Terry?"

"He's down there tending to his dogs. Jaco was hurt pretty bad. They might have to put him under."

Gale was in a fit and started praying. She remembered Dave when he first wandered into the church fresh off the streets. A former Vietnam Vet, disillusioned and trying to adjust to the post-war era, he had tried to drink the nightmares away. It was her idea to hire him as a night watchman. She bought him both dogs and watched with pride as he trained them, prouder than a prep school mom. She begged God to let everything be alright.

The paramedics gathered around Jaco. He snarled at them protectively. His skin was pulled back from his skull in one flap revealing his teeth. It appeared that his hip was shattered as well. Nearby Kindra kept a constant vigil. A foreman of the construction site had been called to cut through the heavy steel girder that had him pinned down.

"It's no good Dave." Troy, the foreman, shouted over the noise of the arc welder. "Even if I do get this thing cut. It's still going to be too heavy to move without risk of just causing more pain to your animal. I need the crane over here."

"Then we'll do it." Dave said panicking. He flashed back to the killing fields of 'Nam and his wounded friends, friends that he would have done anything for, to save.

Jumpin' Jack pulled up and saw the police cars and the crane being moved. He took in the whole situation from a distance and sprinted over taking the chain from the end of the crane and wrapping it around the girder that had Jaco trapped.

"Troy." He shouted. "You can't lift this thing too far or it will set off an avalanche and crush Jaco. Dave, when we get it up just a little pull Jaco out.

"Yes sir!" Dave replied. he took his jacket and tied it tightly around his wounded dog and pled with God to let it live. Jaco looked at him with trusting eyes knowing his master loved him and was doing everything possible to get him out. Kindra ran over and began to dig around the girder trying to get Jaco out.

"No, Kindra, no." Dave said, admiring the courage of his other dog. "It's okay, We'll get him out."

Troy nursed the crane handle gently and felt it start to rock as the chain stretched taut and began to bear the weight of the steel girders. It pulled forward and began to lift. Jack saw that it was pulling the wrong way. he leaned into the girder and began pushing all two thousand pounds away from the dog. Around him the girders started to tremor and the weight shifted slightly. He glanced behind him and saw Dave drag his dog free. He motioned for Troy to lower the chain and scrambled out of the way as the heavy girders shifted positions.

Dave got in the ambulance and rode with Jaco to the Twenty-Four Hour Animal hospital that had been alerted with a Vet team standing by. They wheeled the dog in and began to operate.

Jumpin' Jack stayed behind to survey the damage to the construction site. Before long Wilbur Tonney was down at the scene. He talked with the investigating officers and managed to secure one of the bullet fragments they had recovered.

"How much of the explosives are gone?" Wilbur questioned the Captain, a large man, Herbert Patillo.

"It looks like about eight sticks. But it doesn't take much of this stuff to create a whole lot of damage. They had been using it to blast this granite to bits. Foreman tells me that only about eight sticks were used to blast this entire crater. Whoever has those explosives is a walking time bomb."

"Officer." Jumpin' Jack commented. "Do you think this could be tied to the Tablets we've got on display? The ones being examined over at the Guggenheim? Somebody could blow the whole place to kingdom come, tablets and all. Maybe we'd better have security tightened."

"Good idea Pastor." The Captain responded. "That would be a likely target especially if the terrorist is out for media coverage."

"I've got to go and check on our night watchman and his dog. Here's my card. My mobile number's on the back. If you have anymore questions don't hesitate."

On the way to the animal hospital Jack called Julie's house and apprised them of the situation. She woke up Ben and her father. They all met in the kitchen to discuss their strategy in light of the new events.

"Maybe we ought to just go with what we've got already, Julie." Ben urged. "We can already prove that no instruments were used to carve the tablets. The grooves of the lettering show no trace metals, unlike the edges. All they show is the molecular change similar to a laser."

"He might be right Jules." her father added. "You can conclusively verify them now. Maybe you need to forget the voice programming. If some madman blows the research center, there's going to be nothing left at all. Besides, the book of Revelation says that the voice of God is as the sound of many waters. How are you ever going to distinguish that. It's almost infeasible no matter how many microprocessors you've got on line."

"You think we should just publish and scrap the rest of the experiment because some Italian terrorist wants to keep us from finding out the truth? I'm sorry Dad. It's good advice. But not good enough for me. We can put additional guards on duty and release the findings we have now but we owe it to the world to find out as much as we can, We're on the cutting edge and I don't want to turn back until we've exhausted every possibility."

"Maybe you're right." Julie's father conceded. "But don't let your determination get you killed."

Ignacio limped into a Walgreens drug store, he nearly stumbled over a wine stupor skeleton of a man whose hand was stretched out to him.

"Mister, got a quarta." The man mumbled throwing Ignacio off guard. "A man's entitled to one last cigarette before he dies isn't he?"

Ignacio bent down and spoke softly to him." How'd you like a last meal as well. You do me a little favor I'll spring for a last meal for you. You just wait right here."

Ignacio bought a suture needle, hydrogen peroxide, gauze bandages and challenged the clerk with a very cold look when the clerk went to say something. Ignacio could not figure it out but it seemed like another presence had fused with his black soul.

"Let me have a carton of those cigarettes too," He commanded, pulling out a roll of bills.

He walked out trying to keep his limp as disguised as possible and found the old man still lying by the door waiting for him. He lifted him up without any struggle leaving the paper bag full of the man's personal treasury lying on the ground beside him.

"Come on fellow." Ignacio spoke. "It's time you had a shower and a good meal."

Ignacio drove to a truck stop and rented a room. he filled the tub and put the old man in it The room had a coffee maker and he started a pot brewing taking the time to pull up his leg and examine the wound. He poured the hydrogen peroxide and watched it bubble and turn white around the puncture marks. He saw the ugly gash from the metal girder and poured more in there. He hoped it would be enough for he had no prescription for antibiotics and didn't want to have to go to a hospital and arouse anyone's suspicions. He threaded the needle and began to sew up the gash. He knew it would leave a wicked scar but didn't care. The pain was therapeutic and it cleared his mind. There was another presence living somewhere in him. He sank lower and lower in his thoughts until he could sense the spirit living and breathing. His body grew charged with energy and he looked down at his leg wound and saw it begin to heal. He let out a laugh in demonic glee and threw his hands up in triumph.

"Whom Zeus would destroy, he first must make mad."

The old man got out of the tub and found a package of cigarettes waiting for him as well as a plate of pancakes and bacon and a steaming pot of hot coffee. He looked around for his coat and clothes and couldn't find them. After eating he settled down into a tranquil sleep.

Ignacio stopped at a Goodwill store to purchase a raincoat, alarm clock, shoes, various items of clothing and took his purchases back to his room at the Renaissance. He was quite sure the old man would be sleeping a while. He had sprinkled sleeping pills in with his food and knew it would be hours before the old man was able to get up.

He stepped out of the elevator door and had the strangest sensation that someone was following him down the hall. He looked for the small piece of tape he had left over the edge of the lock and saw it was disturbed. He drew out the blade he kept in his waist and entered the room. The room was dark and he stopped. He could sense fear in the room. He walked over to the closet and crashed his fist through the door catching Wilbur Tonney directly in the chest. he felt the weight of the heavyset man struggling against the sharp steel blade. But the contest was already decided. Ignacio grabbed his large duffel bag and threw a chair through the window. He bounded across the roof towards the fire exit. He was glad he had checked the floor plans before deciding on his room. Behind him he heard shouts and several shots were fired but he was already on the way down. He was hoping they were shortsighted as government agents usually were when they falsely believed that they had their quarry cornered. He ran two blocks over to his car and saw a police officer coming down the road. He ducked behind a rusted dumpster waiting for the car to pass. He was upset that he had left so many of his tools behind but knew he could improvise.

Julie and Ben were guests of honor at the Reinholds as their engagement had been made public. A host of people were present eating, drinking and speculating on the authenticity of their discovery and wondering what the implications would be. John entered the room very soberly and took them both aside.

"I know this is a big day for both of you. "John spoke. "But I'm afraid the news I have is bad and really can't wait."

"What is it. " Ben challenged. "We can handle it."

"I'm afraid our government can no longer adequately protect you. Wilbur Tonney is dead. He had tracked down Ignacio Robella and was stabbed to death in his room with fifteen other agents on lookout as well. This fellow must be invisible. I'm going to make other arrangements for your safety. The first thing we should do is announce to the guests and get you both to a safe house. A very important man owes me some big favors and although I've never before asked to collect, now seems the appropriate time. Hurry, grab a bag each. Time is of the essence."

Ignacio smiled. His plan in part was going very smoothly, he drug his duffel bag up to the room and began stitching the explosives into the jacket of the homeless man. He checked the food he had left and knew the man had eaten enough sleeping pills to put him out for another eight hours. He wired up the jacket and tested his remote and went to sleep.

He looked up at a toothless black man grinning at him.

"You took my clothes, sonny. I'm not going to be able to walk around naked. Would be terrible besides it's powerful cold."

"I brought you some new clothes. I figured you could help me out some on a delivery job. I got you a carton of cigarettes too."

"I could use a drink. I think I'm getting the DT's." The old man replied "Say why are you doing all this, you some kind of priest or religious person?'

The words cut deeply and took Ignacio aback. If the man only knew that he was a lamb being led to the slaughter he would not think too much of his small kindness.

"No." Ignacio said, not wanting to reveal his identity. "I guess I'm just a good Samaritan. The kind you don't see too often over here."

"Where are you from," the bum asked him fingering a cigarette and trying to strike the match.

"Here let me help you." Ignacio said striking a lighter.

The bum took a puff and sat down on a bed.

"I wasn't always like this." The bum said, trying to muster up some self pride. I used to be a preacher, myself. I guess you can say I fell on some hard times. My wife ran off with one of the deacons, daughter was killed in a drive-by and I started looking for my answers in the bottle instead of the Bible. But I know people and you've got something powerful pulling you away from the Lord. If you don't watch it, it'll swallow you like a dragon, drag you down so deep you can't get out of it's clutches. I might be a drunk but I've spent a whole lot of time thinking and praying, helping others a time or two. I just can't seem to find the path back myself. I've got no one left on this here earth that loves me. I guess I'm hoping the sauce will do me in but all it does is leave me emptier than ever. People come and do their charity thing, but no one looks into my soul and sees me. They just see an old bum."

Ignacio was impervious to his words. the spirit that had taken residence within him was devoid of any kindness or love.

"Maybe death is the best thing for you. Then you can finally find yourself some rest."

The man looked at him strangely wondering what he had in mind.

That Sunday morning, the Church was rocking. Over four thousand were in attendance and extra seats were brought in from the cafeteria to handle the overflow. On the platform a singer named Israel was jamming, rocking the house.

"Let's all..., Let's all praise the Lord.
Give God the glory.
Come lift your souls.
There's a song in every heart
Everyone can sing.
Give God the Glory.
Jesus Christ is King."

In front to the platform several people started jumping up and down, clapping their hands. The fervor spread throughout the house. People started falling over as the power of God hit the place like a tornado. The choir on the platform began coming down and praying for people. Jumpin' Jack got worked up and began moving his huge frame around and around. His hands were lifted and his long hair was flying. Israel picked up the tempo and began to dance behind his keyboard, his feet moving like locomotive wheels. People started running the aisles and it looked like the Boston Marathon. Jack Dunlop, in church for the first time, looked over at

Holli who grasped his hand and pulled him with her towards the melee in the front. He felt as if he were running into a heat wave. He couldn't explain it, every cell in his body started to tingle and the hairs on the back of his head stood up straight. He looked and he could see a tall majestic being with huge wings standing behind the singer. He saw a ray of bright light emanating from the windows behind the choir loft. Inside him a voice started speaking to him. He fell unconscious under the power and was unable to move a muscle. Several ushers drug him to the side where he laid, oblivious to his surroundings. His spirit was in another dimension.

He saw himself walking towards the bright light and he approached a large pyramid shaped structure. The bottom layers were a rainbow of translucent stones. It was inset with the largest pearls he had ever seen. They were so tall he couldn't even see the tops of them. He felt compelled to go inside and as he approached the gate he looked down and saw he was wearing tattered garments stained and covered with blood, dirt, excrement. He suddenly felt unworthy and became acutely aware of his many faults and he thought about the destruction he had planned for the Ten Commandments. He knew he had to change course. No matter what the cost, he had to go back to the Rainbow City. He knew it was where he wanted to spend eternity. In the distance he heard laughing and joyful music. He could feel his body again and he slowly regained consciousness. He got up slowly, a bit disoriented and looked over at Holli who was standing with her hands in the air.

The crowd returned to their seats for the message. Jack stumbled back reeling as if he had been drunk.

"The message is from the book of Isaiah. Though your sins be as scarlet, I will make them white as snow."

Jumpin' Jack paused letting the full effect of the words hit home.

"Please," He said sensing the restlessness." I'm going to ask everyone to remain seated for the duration of the message. No running around. I don't want you distracting anyone else. There are lost souls in the house today. Souls that need to hear this message.

"You see. You can't go to Heaven trusting in your good deeds. No. The Bible says that we are all sinners and the soul that sins shall die. You can't get to Heaven based on your good deeds. The Bible says that even the best each of us does is as a filthy rag. You can't go to Heaven because your mom or grandmother was a Christian. Each one of us shall individually give an account for all our deeds.

"So many of you are asking me. 'Jack. How can I get there from here?' There is only one way. It's the way Jesus took. The way of the cross. Jesus told us. "Deny yourself and follow me." That's right. You can jump around until people think you're Carl Lewis at the Olympics or Dennis Rodman rebounding, but jumpin' around doesn't mean a thing except you're a jumpin' fool. You can shout yourself crazy like some trash talking Charles Barkley, but shouting is only going to make you hoarse. You can dance like you're Fred Astaire or Michael Jackson. You can tap dance, line dance, hip hop, boogie woogie, break dance, ballroom dance but you're not going to waltz your way into heaven.

"You're not going to give your way into Heaven either. You can give to the United Negro College Fund, World Vision, Children's Relief, Compassion, St.Vincent's Food Bank, United Way but I'm telling you today, Jesus is the Only way. He's the truth and the light and you ain't going to Heaven unless you go through Him. He went the way of the cross.

"'Father.' He said. 'Take this cup from me, but nonetheless, let not my will be done but yours.'

"A lot of people will tell you, 'come to our church, you can give a big offering and never have to change.' You can cheat the welfare lady by living with your old man behind their backs, but the Bible still calls it fornication. You've got to deny yourselves. Walk the higher path, the path of right doing.

"People will tell you that you don't have to change. God loves you just the way you are. No. He doesn't. God loved us when we were sinners but he doesn't want us to stay sinners. He wants to make us white as snow. Jesus told us the parable about the king who invited everyone to the feast. He couldn't get any of the wealthy people to show up, they were too busy. He couldn't get any of the merchants, they were buying too much and taking inventory of their possessions; so, he sent his servants to the streets. They got the beggars, ragamuffins, homeless and brought them. They were all given a new white garment to wear at the feast. One man didn't put on his garment. He insisted on keeping his own rags. The King told his servants to throw that man out into the darkness where there would be weeping and gnashing of teeth.

"Heaven is, first and foremost, God's house. He has a right to tell us what to wear in his house and a right to let in who He wants, based on the conditions He sets. Just like you tell your visitors to take off their dirty shoes before they tramp on your nice clean carpet. God tells those who are full of sin to stay out of His house. Right next door to us the Institute is housing the original Ten Commandments. How many of them have you broken? Did you ever say. 'Oh God.' If you did you've broken one of them. Did you ever say, 'I wish I had a dress like hers.' Then you've broken another one. Did you ever tell your parents they were crazy or fools or call someone else a fool? Let me assure you, you have broken at least one and that means you have broken them all.

"You know what? God is not surprised. He expected us to break them. He knew we were weak. He knew we were sinners. He talked to Adam and Eve face to face, they still betrayed him. He helped David kill a lion, a bear, a giant of a man, and he still committed adultery with someone else's wife. He helped Peter walk on water and he still denied Christ. God knows you are a sinner made of dust. But get up, put on the armor of God. Put on the mind of Christ, put away the old sinful man. Quit making excuses, lying out of the side of your mouth, telling everybody you're doing your best. Who are you fooling? Not God. He knows every thought, every word, every deed. You might as well come clean now. The day is coming when you are going to have to give an account for everything you've said and done. I mean it. Everything.

"I'm going to stand before God and give an account for calling a person a fool. Even if he was one. I'm not his judge, God is. I'm going to stand accountable for working on the Sabbath Day. I'm going to stand accountable for refusing to help someone I could have helped, for turning the other way when they needed me. You think you're going to have it any easier? The only way God is going to let you off the hook is if you get on the cross. That's right. Get on the cross with Jesus. Deny yourself. Turn from those sins. God loves you. He's paid for all of them, but you've got to take care of them His way."

Jack Dunlop was the first one to come down front. He dropped to his knees in front of the whole congregation and began to sob. Leroy came out of the choir and put his arm around him and began to pray. It was a prayer heard in Heaven. Far beyond where Jack could see. His name was being added to the Book of Life, a name that no one would blot out.

CHAPTER THIRTEEN
Sound Around The World

Jack sat in the room with Leroy, one of the project, engineers helping him with some calculations.

"Who'd have ever thought we would have found the Ten Commandments and been able to prove them real?"

"It doesn't seem like you proved it conclusively yet" Jack answered. "Even if you could figure out the frequency that God spoke in, how are you going to remove all the ambient noise. you can't just filter out several thousand years of noise. I used to do music recording. It's hard to take out the sound of a lyric sheet ruffling in front of a microphone. If these tablets were real they were carried around in battlegrounds, celebrations, rivers, thunderstorms. They've been exposed to every frequency audible and inaudible.

"I figured we'd calculate out the ambient noise in gradations. Even though there is no audible signal being heard. The original vibrations of God's voice are still oscillating, and are most likely to be the oldest signals contained in the stone. So all we have to do is separate out the oldest signal and match it up to the dialogue disks that Dr. Benjamin made for us which we can adapt to any and all frequencies."

"Haven't you already proved that the granite particles in the engraving have been altered by a tremendous heat. Why even go into the audio realm."

"It's there." Leroy spoke smugly." There would be no scientific discoveries if there were no curious scientists."

He was disturbed by the ringing of the phone and swung his chair over to grab it. "I'm here alone with Jack." He answered. "Oh, I understand. Yes. Well, Holli has gone to get us something to eat. She decided to call in sick and spend the rest of the week up here with Jack."

He hung up the phone. "It was Julie. Wilbur Tonney is dead."

"And." Jack added.

"He was the special agent that brought them safely back to the States. Some lunatic is trying to kill them and destroy the Ark as well."

"I know." Jack offered. "Ignacio Robella from the Holy See of Rome. A misguided soul at best an evil man at worst. He will stop at nothing. I suggest you download your data as of now."

"You mean publish it now?"

"Yes." Jack answered. "It's your only protection. Once it has been published it will be too late. Now is the only time."

Leroy looked at him with a puzzled look." You know this guy don't you?"

"He hired me to work for him, but I've changed my mind or

rather God changed my mind for me. Look just send it onto the Internet, you've got a website right?"

"Yes. " Leroy looked at him puzzled." Look how do I know you're not still working with him?"

"Would I have helped you out if I was? Look if this guy is on the move we'll be lucky to get out of here alive."

The array of data was extensive and it took Leroy fifteen minutes to transfer it all on the website. He also sent it by E-mail to Smithsonian magazine and Scientific America. Just as he was finishing, Holli showed up with a large pizza pie and a bag full of drinks.

"What going on?" She said watching Leroy remove the cover over the tablets." I thought you weren't supposed to touch these."

"He doesn't wish to see them get destroyed."

"By whom?" She was puzzled. "Look is anybody going to have some pizza? I had to drive halfway to Dearborn to find decent pizza, now you're both leaving?"

"If we don't leave now we're apt to be buried with our pizza." Jack responded. "Holli, I was hoping I could avoid the subject but I can't. I was hired by a member of the Holy See to make sure none of this documentation ever got out to the scientific community. Now an FBI agent is dead, explosives are missing and there's a good chance they were stolen to destroy this building and it's contents. So we're clearing out. Why don't you help us? We need to disguise these tablets and get them out of here."

Ignacio watched from a stolen Detroit Edison van. He had finally broken down and bought the old man a bottle and was allowing him to greedily swallow a few drops in hopes of keeping him on the wire. Due to the substantial contribution by the church community to the Guggenheim Foundation a subterranean passageway had been built between the two structures. Ignacio had examined the building permits and knew just where the explosives should be placed to bring the maximum structural damage. He was relieved to see no guards posted but knew they could be anywhere.

He was hoping his true intention to destroy the tablets was unknown.

"Let's go." He motioned to the old man. he placed a yellow hard-hat on him. "There you look like part of the team."

Ignacio had wired five explosive devices that he had intended to put around the main structural support of the science foundation.

A staff member greeted him as he entered the church.

"Can I help you sir?" The man asked.

"Yes." Ignacio smiled. "We need to fix a junction box along the passageway."

"Just follow down the hall, you'll see the stairway and the sign to the science foundation."

"Thanks.'"

Leroy tugged at the cart holding the tablets. Holli was carrying a box of handwritten notebooks, eating a piece of pizza. Jack stopped when he heard a fire alarm. Leroy turned.

"Just a hunch. " Jack said." But I think we've got an unwanted guest."

Ignacio cursed as he heard the fire alarm go off. He knew he had only minutes and wondered if he'd be able to get away on time.

"That's a fire alarm son. I think we'd better get back outside." the bum addressed him.

The old man turned and began to walk back. Ignacio ignited in fury and reached out and smashed him across the face breaking his jaw. The old man was in shock.

Before he could faint from the pain Ignacio hit him with a powerful uppercut that knocked the wind out of him. The priest's powerful hands drug him down the passageway and left him lying in a heap while the priest broke the security door setting off another series of alarms almost unnoticeable in the din created by the first set.

The Guggenheim was arrayed as a large circular building with hallways at the outer perimeters and the offices and lab set in the middle. People dubbed the hallway as the track. As Holli, Jack and

The Voice

Leroy pushed the cart towards the passageway doors back towards the church they heard moaning. Holli rushed over and saw the bum. He had been chained and locked to the post. Barely conscious, he was moaning in pain.

Jack pushed them aside and examined him then felt his chest.

"This man is a bomb." He exclaimed." Get out of here both of you."

Jack." Holli said unsure of whether or not to run for it or stay with him. "We can't leave him.'

"It'll do you no good to die with him. I'll go back to the lab and get one of the saws. I think I'll be able to cut him loose. Anyway if I don't..."

Jack's voice echoed down the hall as he ran back to find some equipment to release the man before his body was scattered all over the hallway.

Ignacio stood in the hallway looking for the supports that kept the building up, he pulled out his C-4 explosives and dropped them next to a large steel pole. He kept circling, dropping off the other explosives setting the timers to go off like a grand finale fourth of July explosion, bringing the building and contents into total oblivion. A voice told him to cut into one of the offices. When he did so he heard someone rumbling around.

Jack had dug out the tool chest and was getting an extension cord to power the small diamond blade saw he wanted to use to cut the old man free. He glanced over and saw he was being watched. The glow from the exit light gave Ignacio an ethereal appearance as if he were a deadman come back to life.

Ignacio stepped into the light gun drawn.

"I thought you always completed your jobs. you've disappointed me Mr. Dunlap." He motioned and directed him with the tip of his gun. "Move over there slowly and if you try to be a hero you'll find yourself a dead one.'

"Do you know you're trying to destroy the Ten Commandments?" Jack questioned. "You really think you can stand against the written word of God and triumph?"

"Yes." Ignacio." I think God's already lost. It's up to us to collect the spoils, and if some religious artifact gets destroyed in the process then that's just part of the process."

Jack looked around for someplace to hide as he turned his head Ignacio brought his gun down swift and hard on the side of his temple sending him into unconsciousness. Ignacio drug his body over by another support pole and propped it up, a placing neat bundle of C-4 and dynamite in his lap. He looked down on his body.

"I told you, you'd be sorry if you ever crossed me."

Leroy waited outside with Holli wondering if Jack was going to make it out okay.

"We can't just leave him there Leroy." Holli spoke. "I'm going back in. God help me."

"The explosives." Leroy protested struggling with the decision.

"God can handle the explosives." She said marching back towards the science foundation.

"Wait," Leroy said, his throat dry from panic. "I think I can dismantle that fuse."

Leroy took some small tools out of the box he was carrying and went to the downstairs door. He pushed the entry code placed his palm print on the locking device and the door slid open. Holli was impressed by the high tech stuff but just followed him quietly.

The power was out and the corridors glowed with the red exit signs. Holli's heart was racing rapidly her high heels clicking against the floor. Leroy heard a clank and stopped. He motioned to her to remove her shoes. She did and they both heard a moaning coming from the research lab.

They spotted Jack leaned up against a pole with a load of explosive taped to his chest. He was outfitted with a crude timing device which took Leroy all of about one minute to disconnect. His face was turning purple and he was only semiconscious.

"Help me lift him will you. There were only four minutes left on that timing clock and if we don't get him out of here soon. There will be nothing left."

Outside several fire trucks pulled up. Ignacio was wearing the Detroit Edison uniform and approached one of the firemen as he came to the entrance.

"Just a malfunctioning alarm. "He spoke looking nervously about. "It must have tripped when I was working on the transformer over there.'

"Just the same we've got to clear the building." The fireman answered.

Several other firemen joined him and they entered the side of the building where Leroy had left it open. They bumped into Holli dragging the body of Jack out and immediately lifted him up with her.

"There's an old man tied up with explosives. One of the scientists is trying to get him loose. Hurry there's only a few minutes until the bombs are rigged to go."

Ignacio watched from the Edison Van. He decided it was time for him to make his exit and turned the ignition switch. The van wouldn't start. Police sirens were heard in the distance and Ignacio watched as a cruiser pulled in back of him. A large bomb truck pulled up and parked adjacent to him blocking his exit. He watched Jack carried to a waiting ambulance. The speed in which the emergency crew responded amazed him. The officer in charge of the bomb squad lost control of the German Shepherd which ran over towards him and was barking. Ignacio started to make his exit on foot heading for a small clump of trees in the park across the street. The dog went crazy pulling the work bag out of his arms. Ignacio threw it to the ground. Unfortunately he had caught the attention of several police officers.

"You, Stop. " One of the officers cried out.

Ignacio looked around and changed directions. He looked up a moment before a large ambulance turning the corner came right into his path of escape. The ambulance hit him squarely in the midsection. He was thrown ahead of the vehicle and felt the tires pass over his legs as his bones were crushed in hundreds of shards.

The dog tore apart the bag and the officer could see the C-4 and several remaining sticks of dynamite. The contents were delicately carried to the bomb truck.

In the building the minutes ticked away as Leroy, sweating feverishly, sawed through the chain which held the old man to the pole. Just as he cut through the last part of the link several emergency workers saw him and came to his aid.

"There's only about sixty seconds on the timer." Leroy said his voice cracking with the stress.
"I think I can disarm it."

"It's not worth it. There's probably others. Just get out of here. We got him."

Leroy took off running for the door. The firemen picked up the body of the old man and carried him down the hall. They were almost at the door when the first explosion hit. It knocked them off their feet but they were able to pick the old man up and make it out the door before the second third and forth explosions hit. The crowd outside witnessed the Science Foundation collapsing like a wedding cake layer by layer. The explosive devices took out enough of the main support to bring down the floors above and the roof.

"They caught him. They caught him!" Holli shouted to Jack, just beginning to recover.

"Caught who?" He answered as an approaching vehicle drew his attention. "Looks like Julie and Ben."

"Holli." Julie said." I heard you guys were in there with Leroy. Did everyone get out?"

"Leroy gave us your files and stayed to help this old man who was chained up. Jack got clobbered pretty bad."

"That's him over there. The Vatican bomber. Same guy that blew up the museum in Israel. I recognize his face. Jack was working for him."

The Voice

"Holli." Jack said exasperated. "I probably would have completed my contract but I don't usually work for people who blow buildings up and murder people. I'm in industrial espionage. At least I was. Now I've got to follow the Ten Commandments, seeing as how God wrote them."

"Julie. "Ben spoke." There's Leroy. it looks like he got out okay. Glad you made it out Jack, but I think someone is even happier than me." He pointed to Holli.

"Maybe the two of you can come to our wedding." Ben smiled. "What do you say.'

"I'd be crazy to turn down an invitation from the world's most eminent archaeologist. Sure where is it?"

"Jerusalem." Ben smiled at his trickery. "Next month. Thanks for your help. I got the e-mail. You could have destroyed everything but you didn't."

"I don't think He" Jack pointed towards the sky. "Would have allowed it. Obviously He wanted those tablets and the Ark discovered. I'm going to look in on Ignacio."

Jack went over to the ambulance and looked at Ignacio lying on a stretcher. Tubes were sticking out of his arms and the EMT team had put splints on his legs and a neck brace on him. As Jack looked him in the eyes, he could see a red glow emanate and evil presence seemed to speak to him. Ignacio burst out of his arm restraint and reached for his throat. A strong guttural sound burst forth from his throat.

"You will die Jack Dunlap." The voice spoke as the hands tried to squeeze his throat.

Jack reacted in horror, pulling back trying to get away. Unseen by him another presence enfolded him with a warm supernatural light. His guardian angel stepped forth and cast off the spirit of darkness seeking to destroy him.

"You have no authority Rothar." The angel of light spoke.

"And you do, Zoe?" Rothar replied loosening the grip on Jack's throat. "He'll be mine soon enough even as this one is."

The Voice

"Only one Being knows the end of these humans and it is not the being that rules your domain. It is the Lord glorious and lifted up. Praise be unto His name. He alone commands light and darkness. You speak as one foolish." Zoe corrected, nudging Jack to leave the emergency vehicle.

Jack watched as Ignacio's body was driven away, and pondered his judgment in entering into any kind of business deal with one so evil.

The publishing of the documents on the Ten Commandments stirred up more controversy than any other Archeological or Scientific discovery in history. Noted scholars took it upon themselves to discredit the findings of the GUGGENHEIM TEAM and wrote lengthy articles and appeared on talk shows in every major country citing the discovery as the work of "lunatics," "religious fanatics," and "frauds." Ben was besieged with requests to rebut many of the arguments and chose to accept a national debate with a scientist from the Anthropology Department from Princeton.

He flew to Newark Airport with Julie and Leroy and they drove out to Princeton in a roomy rental from Budget.

"You sure you want to do this Ben?" Leroy asked. "You don't have to explain yourself to anyone. The facts speak for themselves."

"Ben." Julie added. "I'm worried about you. American scientists don't have a record for playing fair."

"Look." Ben added, driving by the expanse of oak and maple trees turning orange and red in the afternoon autumn sun. "People have been denying the right of God to rule their lives since Adam and Eve. I don't know what they're going to throw at me, but I know God's going to help me with the answers I need. I don't know how, but I know He will. So let them throw bricks at me, let them throw bricks at our research. I just hope that those watching will have their consciences pricked and know that mankind is not a law unto himself. There is a Creator and Judge of us all, and unless we can meet each requirement of His law, we will perish. 'Thy law have I hid in my heart, that I may not sin against Thee.' So, thanks for your concern, but you two both did a great job of documenting your research... I don't think this guy has any real ammunition to throw."

On the thirteenth floor of the Henry Ford Hospital ICU, Ignacio slipped deeper and deeper into a coma. His mind was tormented by Rothar and a host of spirits and he wasn't even conscious when the surgeon had removed both of his legs leaving him with stumps from the hip down. He lay alone as one dead, the police having abandoned guarding him when they realized he was permanently immobilized.

Worldwide Outreach Center intercession team had taken up praying for Ignacio and from time to time several of the women would go to the hospital and visit him. They were praying for a complete recovery. The Vatican had gone on record denouncing him as a rogue and fanatic, and took no responsibility for his actions.

The young Monsignor, Father Sulleizi, walked down the giant hallway to the Cardinal's Office. He was a relatively young man amongst the aged church leader who were all pushing seventy. A Jesuit by training, Sulleizi felt no tolerance for those who disagreed with the basic tenants of the Holy Mother church. To him protestants, though Christian in name, were as far removed from God as any other infidel. He stopped to look at an oil painting done by Raphael depicting the casting down of Satan to Hell and smiled. The enemies of the church would ultimately go to hell as well and he would sit with others of his faith, the true followers of Peter at the side of Christ. His heart was overflowing with self-righteous pride as he opened the massive oak door and stepped into the opulent office, lavishly decorated with furniture as old as Charlemagne and Michelangelo. The wealth of the church never ceased to amaze him. He felt as if it were a part of him. As an employee would have pride in his corporation, Sulleizi knew the Holy Mother Church's holdings would put even the largest

The Voice

corporations to shame.

"Sit down father." The raspy voice behind the huge Italian renaissance desk spoke to him. "Would you care for a cigar or some brandy? You'll find some on the table beside your chair, it's best if my identity remains a secret to you in case during this mission you find yourself detained. On official record, this meeting, this conversation never took place. Do you understand father?" The voice continued.

Sulleizi didn't have the vaguest idea who it was talking to him. "Yes." He replied.

"Now in the folder next to you, go ahead, take a minute to examine the contents, you will find a plane ticket, a thousand dollars in American currency, and a small package with a hypodermic needle. I know you were once in the medical corp so I'm sure you know how to use it."

"Yes." Sulleizi replied. "Who is it I am supposed to use it on?"

"You are aware of the embarrassment Father Ignacio Robella has been to the Holy Mother Church? Well, certain parties want to make sure he never comes out of his coma. There's a special desire that he keeps his vow of silence. One injection will insure that. Don't worry, you are not administering a lethal injection. Let's just say, that this injection will ensure and help him keep his vow of silence and not bring any further disgrace on us. It's for the greater good of the Church's work amongst our Jewish brethren. We cannot let them see that we envy their hold on the promised land - the very birthplace of our Lord Jesus Christ and His Holy Mother Mary."

Sulleizi wondered at his fortune at being picked for such a sacred mission. He knew of Robella, "Voltura" they had nicknamed him because of his balding dome. He had studied him and read many of his canons on the defense of the faith. Many believed his views contradicted the spirit of ecumenicalism that had invaded much of the thinking of the church but Sulleizi was not one of those who favored peace with infidels. To him, there was only one Holy Mother Church, and whoever was not in the fold was a bastard child.

Sulleizi felt the cold Atlantic air chilling him as he traveled on the non-stop between Rome and JFK. He thought of the Jesuit Priests that had come before him to establish works amongst the Indians and had so often paid with their lives. He didn't know how Ignacio had disgraced the church and wanted to learn more about him. In particular, he wanted to know who he worked for and who had given him the idea to destroy the Ten Commandments and the Ark. Why anyone in the church hierarchy would want to destroy a valuable relic was beyond him. He thought of the pieces of the cross he had kissed and the hair and bones of St. Peter, St. Thomas and how much they meant to all the faithful. He dismissed the thoughts. When he had tried to find out more about Ignacio, no one was talking. Even his mentor Cardinal Hofstradt from Germany, a good friend of the Pope, had told him to mind his own business. What were they all hiding?

His attention turned to the sight of New York City as they circled the Statue of Liberty and landed harshly, bumping up and down. He was aware of the stares by those who were uncomfortable around a man of the collar and laughed at their pitiful attempts of piousness. It accorded him a certain amount of respect amongst the church's faithful at least, and on many occasions he found that his bills for meals were simply taken care of.

The flight to Detroit took less than two hours. By the time he had checked into his hotel he was weary from all his travels and took a hot bath and went to bed. He woke up to the sound of jackhammers outside breaking up an old concrete foundation. The phone rang.

"Father." The voice spoke. "This is the front desk. Your 'do not disturb' light is on but someone on the phone is insisting that it's urgent. Would you like us to patch the call through?"

"Yes." He answered, rubbing the crust from his eye. "Go ahead."

"You know who this is. "The mysterious voice from the

The Voice

Vatican spoke.

"No." He thought aloud. "I mean I don't know who you are but I recognize the voice from before."

"Good, then listen. There's been a slight change of plans. When you leave the room of your target, make sure there are no vital signs. None. There is another packet we weren't originally planning on using, it's blue. Inject it into his IV and wait in the room until all signs of life disappear."

The phone went dead and Sulleizi looked at the receiver like it was a bad joke and put it back on the cradle.

"Holy Mother of God." He muttered abstractly making the sign of the cross.

"Who do they think I am?" He wondered, getting up out of bed. "Silence is a far different thing than death."

He felt a heaviness come over him as he stood in the threshold of decision -whether or not to take the life of another man. A life sacred to God and God alone.

He thought of his vows as a priest, vows made in the presence of God, the Ten Commandments, and could find no way in his mind to justify what they were telling him to do. He pushed it out of his mind with a long hot therapeutic shower, draining the evil from his pores and letting his mind wander out on a thousand different tangents. Like a humanoid, he mechanically got dressed, took his black bag and went downstairs. A cabdriver was waiting. Hanging from the fellows mirror was a color print of Christ on a cross.

"Good morning Father." The cab driver spoke. "Look like it's going to be a great day. Where to?'

He handed the man the card to the hospital. Not wishing to start a conversation.

The cab driver was undaunted and went on talking a thousand miles an hour. Sulleizi just nodded and replied with an occasional grunt and stepped out of the cab to pay his fare. The cab driver looked at him.

The Voice

"Some things in life other people can't tell you what to do. You just have to decide for yourself." He handed Sulleizi the fare back. "When you make the right choice you never regret it. Have a good day father."

The priest inquired about the ICU and went up to the floor where Ignacio was being kept. Several orderlies were pushing carts around. No one that saw him gave much of a reaction. The room was unmarked and Sulleizi could see the one-half figure lying on an elevated hospital bed. He went up for a close look and saw there was no movement. He took Ignacio's hand and felt the side of his temple. There was a pulse but ever so faint. Sulleizi pulled back the covers and gasped in horror. Two white bandages were wrapped at the bottom of his hips. There were no legs. Sulleizi remembered the scripture about it better having your legs cut off than suffering the fires of hell with your legs if they offended God. He was moved to pity and began to weep. He heard a ruffling and looked in the corner. There was an old black man dressed in a plain brown suit.

"I wanted to kill him too." The man spoke. "He left me tied up in that Science foundation with enough TNT in my lap to launch me clear to the moon. But now. I just come in and pray for him. When I was tied up there I had a chance to really think and pray. Well, God brought me down to the wire but brought me through. That man was his instrument. You're here to kill him aren't you?"

"Why..." Sulleizi stuttered. Amazed that he had been found out so completely.

"It's all right. I told you I wanted to kill him too. He got his punishment. Look at him, no legs. Why do you want to take his life from him too? Maybe this will be the chance he needs to save his soul. Maybe him losing his legs was the best thing ever happened to him. What about you? You want to walk around the rest of your life knowing you killed one of God's creation? Branded like Cain who killed his own brother. I don't think you need that, do you?"

"How'd you know?" Sulleizi asked honestly. "Why are you here?"

The Voice

"I come in everyday praying for him. I've been waiting for you, saw you in my dreams. I couldn't just let you send this man to Hell. Look at him, he's tormented. Look at how twisted up and distorted his face is. He already thinks he's in Hell because he can't wake up. Demons have him bad. I don't know what He did but I wouldn't want to be where he's at. Would you?"

"No." Sulleizi mumbled. "What am I going to tell them?"

"The church people, right? That's who told you to do this? They won't get the blood on their own hands so they get someone else to do it. I think it's time you changed churches, Father. Time to join the Church of Brotherly love. It's the only church that matters to Him. Not creed or doctrine or outward garments but what's in here." He pointed to his chest.

"You mean just not return?"

"Stay here in Detroit. There's plenty of work to do, why in this hospital alone there's over five hundred beds and every soul close to eternity."

"A rogue priest." Sulleizi laughed. "Don't suppose I have much of a choice. Whoever wanted me to do this is not going to look too kindly on my disobedience."

The old man reached in and gave him a card. "We've got an old parsonage right down the street next to the Methodist Church. You're welcome to use it. Ladies will come by, do your washing, cooking. You stay here awhile."

"Really?" Sulleizi was touched. He held the card as if it were a priceless gemstone. "Thanks, I will."

"And don't worry about your finances," The old man added, as Sulleizi left the room. "God's got a way of providing for his own."

Ignacio stirred in his coma, aware that forces were trying to pull him back from hell. It felt as if he were being torn apart. In his heart and with all his will he began to pray. For mercy, for peace, for another chance at life. He knew when he got out things would be different.

Sulleizi never checked back into his hotel room. He had his

savings transferred to Chase Bank and simply disappeared. The mysterious voice could never find him. No address, no phone, just a man on a mission from God, but this time his mission was different. No more defending worthless doctrines of man and petty religious differences - he was on a mission of love.

He was tireless in his visiting of the sick, the poor. Children followed him through the streets like he was the pied piper. He always had an extra stick of gum or piece of candy. He chose to keep his vow of celibacy made from his heart to the heart of God but was never lacking for dinner invitations or parties. He kept his background a secret from everyone. They knew him only as Father Don. When people looked in his eyes, they saw the eyes of a God who was compassionate, kind and loving. In time his clerical outfit grew tattered and he just made his rounds dressed in a colorful jogging suit and shoes. He helped get scholarships for many of the inner-city kids who had no fathers. He became a father to the fatherless beseeching foundations and wealthy benefactors for scholarship money. It could be said that no one in his neighborhood went to bed hungry or not knowing they were loved. Father Don made sure of that.

It was six months to the day that Ignacio recovered, and the demons that plagued him left. The prayers and petitions of God's people saw to that. Father Don, with the help of Jumpin' Jack and some very influential politicians, had him released into his custody. They sent him to Phoenix to a specialist who outfitted him with working artificial legs. Not a word was heard from the Vatican. His bills were paid in full and Ignacio Robella never had to stand trial for any of his murders. The gun found with his prints in Jerusalem mysteriously disappeared and there were no eyewitnesses for the death of Wilbur Tonney either. The one who forgives all had forgiven him and laid another course for his life.

The Temple's inner Sanctuary was rebuilt according to the plans God had given Solomon. Ben and Julie who had taken up residence in Jerusalem attended. Ben found a teaching position with a Christian University which specialized in Biblical Archaeology. He loved his job and was happily married to Julie, who had taken a position with an Israeli software manufacturer.

"You know Ben." Julie stated. "They wouldn't be having this dedication today if you hadn't found the Ark."

"Well." Ben explained. "I think it's more because God wanted it found. I just happened to be in the right place to be used to find it. Besides it wasn't just me, your brother pushed me right along, always telling me not to give up. You still miss him don't you?"

"Yeah." Julie said. "In a way I feel like he sacrificed his life for us so we could meet. Look over there, people are already lined up."

"There's over four million visitors. People from every country of the world have come to see this Temple being dedicated. It's bigger than the Olympics. They gave us special credentials and a special area to in. I hope we're not too late."

"I hope the terrorists have all decided to stay home.'

Ben maneuvered their BMW down a small side street to the lot adjacent to the Temple. It was a magnificent structure. Over five billion dollars in donations had come in making it the most expensive building ever built in modern history. The government of South Africa had donated all the gold. Italy had donated all the marble as reparation for taking part in the World War. England had donated all the lumber and structural designs and India had donated most of the rugs and tapestries. Wealthy American Jews had sent over at least fifty billion dollars and several of the developers had built the worker's housing. A crew of over five thousand had worked on the structure day and night for a year, with many of the structural pieces completed off site and brought in by helicopter and truck. It was the most monumental structural achievement the world had ever seen.

They could hear the chorus of voices as the choir, over ten thousand strong, performed along with ancient instruments. Songs were reconstructed from ancient melodies. A pathway of flowers was strewn from the Knesset throughout the city. People were lined up to see the procession of the Ark that would make it's way back to the Holy of Holies. Dancers with timbrels leapt in joy, accompanied by the cheering of the multitudes as the Ark made it's way down some of the small streets towards the expansive courtyard area.

Ben and Julie had a seat on the platform where the Ark was to be dedicated by the new High Priest right after several bulls were sacrificed on the bronze altar. Julie could hear the large animals moving about. There was also a small flock of white lambs that were to be sacrificed at the same time. Her mind went to the sacrifice of Christ, the Lamb of God, and she wondered why so many in the Jewish Orthodox religion couldn't make the connection between the two. She took Ben's hand and squeezed. Finally, their wait was over. The din of the crowd grew so loud one would have thought they were standing under a powerful waterfall. As the Ark made it's final passage up the great steps that led to the Temple courtyard, a hush grew over the crowd. Although it was mid-day, no one had predicted a total eclipse of the sun. The sky grew dark, and in the distance, thunder could be heard. Many people drew close together, frightened and perplexed. There was a bright light that shown down on the Ark as if a spotlight beyond the dimensions of the physical universe was beamed down from somewhere out in space. Cameras quit rolling, all the voices quieted, anxiously awaiting the supernatural visitor. A thunderous sound enveloped the crowd, creating a tremor in the very ground upon which they all were standing. The Temple began to sway, its architectural structure built on huge rubber plates gave in to the swaying and rolling motion of the earth Everyone watched spellbound, not understanding the mysterious visitation.

"I am the Lord." The voice spoke. Each one listening heard it in their own language, the sound sweeping through the air around them. "I dwell not in Temples made by human hands but in the spirit of love within each one of you. You have before you the original laws as given to my servant Moses and your forefathers who wandered through the Sinai for over forty years because of their unbelief. Now look everyman in his heart and you will see a new law, yes, even one My own hand has written, not on a tablet of stone, as sits before you here, but on your very conscience. Don't pass by one who is hungry without giving that one food. Don't pass by one who is thirsty without giving that one drink. Don't pass by one naked without giving clothing. Love others with the same love which you love yourself and love me with all your heart, soul, mind and strength. You have brought before Me animals for sacrifice, but I have become a sacrifice, yes, in this very city I was led like a lamb to the slaughter and crucified for your sins. I love you my people. I have brought you out of captivity, away from the sword of the Holocaust and have preserved you as a remnant for my sake. I AM YESHUA. I AM THE LORD."

Everyone could hear echoing trumpet sounds and angelic choirs as the eclipse receded and the sun shone once again on the courtyard. People dropped to their knees and begged forgiveness for their selfish lack of love. The High Priest prostrated himself before the Lord and began to weep. It was many hours later when the crowds went back to their hotel rooms and homes. Not a single animal had been sacrificed. In Jerusalem that night not a beggar slept on the streets or went hungry. Those who had come to see the historical tablets had left knowing the true law. The law of love was written deep within them, and all they had to do to live lives pleasing to God, was to follow the very intuition He had placed within each one of them.

The End

EPILOGUE

Detroit was voted "friendliest city in the USA" due to the work of Ignacio and Suzzeili. Foundations donated property for job training, housing, businesses and unemployment dropped to less than one percent in the Detroit Metro Area. The World Outreach Center continued to grow and ended up in a rebuilding program which included a new hockey stadium to house a professional Christian Hockey Team which put on exhibitions year round.

Julie and Ben continued with their research in Jerusalem. Julie became pregnant soon after her wedding and they are now parents of a bouncing baby boy named Benjamin. Their home became a center for all Messianic Jews and they did their best to let people know about Yeshua, the Messiah.

Jack Dunlap payed some massive fines for his industrial espionage, but in his plea bargain he managed to escape any prison time. He went on to marry Holli and started a computer consulting business that helped churches and non-profit organizations set up their own interactive websites.

John Reinjohn and his wife sold all of their worldly possessions and moved to Ethiopia to work in the field with a World Vision feeding program. They make trips several times per year to visit their new grandchild in Israel.